Tony Bury, born 1972 in Northampton, England, has had a passion for writing songs, poems and short stories since an early age. He has taken it more seriously since having kids, writing several children's books and screen plays. *Intervention Needed* is his second novel in the Alex Keaton series, following on from *Intervention Forgiven.*

Intervention Needed

Intervention Needed is the second Alex Keaton novel.

Also by Tony Bury

Intervention Forgiven

Tony Bury

Intervention Needed

Vanguard Press

VANGUARD PAPERBACK

© Copyright 2016
Tony Bury

A CIP catalogue record for this title is
available from the British Library.

ISBN 978 178465 123 7

*Vanguard Press is an imprint of
Pegasus Elliot MacKenzie Publishers Ltd.*
www.pegasuspublishers.com

First Published in 2016

**Vanguard Press
Sheraton House Castle Park
Cambridge England**

Printed & Bound in Great Britain

To Nan. No longer with us.
Thanks for all the bottle returns.

Chapter 1

Alex opened her eyes. She could just about make the break of dawn through the curtains. Her thoughts started to wander, to what another day running on little sleep, and lots of coffee was going to be like. She stretched her arms backwards to find an empty bed. This was a surprise; it hadn't been a normal occurrence since she and Chris returned from Germany.

Chris had stayed over nearly every night or she had stayed at his house. There had been no talk of love or togetherness, just a need for company on both their parts after the events they had been through together in the past two months. It was Chris and the captain that officially broke the news to Alex of Sophie's death.

A break-in was the official line of the investigation. The burglars had managed to go through the belongings in the house and found Paul's gun. They believe Sophie woke up and startled them in the nursery. They shot her at point blank range. There were officers searching for the murder weapon and interviewing the usual suspects but they had very little to go on. Alex was confident they were finding neither. She had changed her gun for Paul's after the shooting, as they had the same model and make and nobody looked at serial numbers. If someone had asked it was highly likely at some point in their partnership they had changed weapons.

The weapon she had used to kill Sophie – her gun – she had thrown into the river the morning of the shooting from the nearest suspension bridge. It was deep and nobody was going to be dragging it up. Her prints had been at the house and she had told them she had met with Sophie the day before, just for a coffee and a chat. Nobody would have had any doubt to trust her; she had been a loyal and trusting friend, up until the day she shot her in cold blood. What was worrying Alex more is the little she felt about what she had done. It was somehow justified in the fact that she knew that a little monster was growing inside her, a monster that thanks to Jack she now had the code to be able to recognise. Paul's little boy was not going to grow up into a Stephen or a Michael.

Michael Mellor had figured a lot in her mind lately, the thought of what he had done and what she had let him get away with. The thought that he was still out there and had those urges. She knew it was only a matter of time before the hunger would take over him again and that she would be on the hunt for him. Michael was a murderer plain and simple.

But that wasn't a thought for today. Today she had to mourn for her lost friend and look convincing in her actions. She needed them all to know how much Sophie had meant to her.

"Morning, Sunshine." Chris brought a tray of coffee into the room.

"Morning." Alex sat up in bed; today wasn't going to be an easy day to get through. "I was thinking about going into the office first. The funeral isn't till one and we have a lot of cases piling up."

Alex didn't want to go to the funeral with Chris. She thought it better to go on her own. This thing that was happening between them, it wasn't a couple thing. It was just two people in need of some fun. She knew he would turn up to support her today; his actions had been different since returning from Germany – more sincere, more caring.

"OK, do you want to ride in together?"

"Don't think so, do you? Nobody knows about us and I would rather keep it that way."

"That's fine, I am your dirty little secret, Miss Keaton."

"You know what I mean." Alex threw on her robe and headed for the shower. "It's not like we have to be together all the time, like now, in the shower – it's not like we can both fit in." She dropped the robe and disappeared out of sight. Chris put down his coffee on the bedside cabinet and followed Alex to the shower.

The car ride into the office was longer than usual, there seemed to be an accident every two miles. Alex had left Chris getting ready at hers after distracting him from awkward conversations with the lure of a shower. She didn't need complications in relationships; there was too much going through her head.

James was sitting at his desk when she walked in. Coffee had been made and left on the table. "I didn't say I was coming in this morning"

"You didn't have to, I knew you wouldn't take half a day off. Anyway now we are both back on full responsibilities, the work load piling up, I knew you couldn't ignore it."

James was right. Alex couldn't ignore anything that had been going on, but she was seeing this in a different perspective now. It wasn't as simple as violent behaviour or murder. There were other factors to consider, other factors like where they were born for instance.

Something still only she knew about. Something she wasn't yet willing to share with her partner or her fellow law enforcers. Not yet. Jack had led her down the path and now she held the key to knowing a murderer.

"So which case are we starting with, or is that a silly question?"

Alex picked the files off her desk and started to sort through them. "Well we have an apparent suicide, a violent drunk driver and by all accounts a cold blooded murder."

"So the suicide then? We seem to be good at them. And let's face it, you never know where it might lead."

James had been teasing Alex about her holiday in Germany with her husband Chris and their soon-to-be love child. It was all a ruse to get into the Brown Institute but funny nonetheless. Alex just smiled at him.

"Murder it is then. The crime scene photos are all in there and I was going to take a ride over to go over the scene one more time before they wrap it up... are you coming?"

"No, you do that, I will start looking at the usual suspects before going over to the church. Make sure you speak to the neighbours and get all their names and the family names of anyone who lives there. I mean it, anyone; brother, sister, cousin, visitors from out of town."

"Okay, okay, hope it goes well, as well as those things can go? You know what I mean."

Alex did know what he meant; she sat at her desk and waited for James to leave the room. As soon as he did she opened her drawer and pulled out the lock box where she was supposed to keep her gun when she was in the office. Opening it with a key from her pocket she removed the hard drive that Dee had given her. Her hands began to shake; this was the first time she had touched it since the night before going to Sophie's. She was scared about the power it had over her, the knowledge that on this hard drive there were potentially hundreds and thousands of killers all committing or about to commit murder. This hard drive is what had ended Jack Quaid's life. His sacrifice, his break-in to the Brown Institute, twice, had given Alex the information she had been searching for.

She loaded it into the computer, and put in the name Jessica Hall. Nothing. She tried again just with the name Hall. There were several, none within a thousand miles of there though and with various stages of ... Alex stopped and thought, various stages of what, what were these people exhibiting?, various stages of behaviour, traits, symptoms. Whatever these people had it was predictable, it was in them and something they couldn't fight. They had been given the gene that would heighten psychopathic tendencies or murderous intent, obsession, loyalty, all things people thought they learnt, to find out it had been placed in them.

Alex was satisfied that the victim wasn't one of them. Jessica Hall had been found in her apartment by a friend. The friend had come over to cook her lunch as a surprise and had the spare key. There were no signs of a break-in to the apartment which led Alex to believe that Jessica knew her killer. She was naked and at one point tied to the bed with silk scarfs, wearing nothing but a blindfold. The ME had said that it looked like rough sex, but there was a belief that it was consensual. What Chris had actually said to Alex was 'I like the scarfs, we should try that'. What wasn't consensual though was the fact that the murderer had taken a small piece of cord and tied it around her neck until she asphyxiated. There was wine on the dining room table and after her murder she was laid out perfectly on the bed, legs together and arms by her side. The murderer had taken his time as if he had some kind of feelings for the victim after he had killed her.

Alex wasn't going to solve this now. The only thing she had that was concrete was the name of the victim. Locking the hard drive away back into the gun box Alex sat back in her chair. Pausing for a minute before leaning forward, she opened the PC back up and typed a name into Google. Michael Mellor. Within seconds, pictures of Michael and Maria appeared on her screen. She sat there looking at them for a while and clicked on the latest posting.

Michael had sponsored the opening of an art gallery in town. He and Maria were there, scissors in hand and smiling for the cameras. Alex could feel herself getting agitated at the picture and the thought of him out and in the population. She knew what he was, and it was only a matter of time before someone else was going to find out in person.

She had sworn to herself that she needed to apprehend Michael. She had let him go to be able to pursue the case, Jack's case. She was working on the bigger picture for the truth but now that she had this, she needed to make sure she corrected her mistakes. Closing the PC down it was time to move on. Sophie was being buried shortly and all her family were going to be there to support her parents through this time. There was another Michael she was going to have to deal with today – Paul's brother. Alex was going to have to look him straight in the eye knowing what she had done. It was going to be hard; especially knowing how much he looked like Paul.

The Mellor household was still quiet. The staff were used to being discreet and seen but not heard, but this morning was exceptionally quiet. Christopher and Carly were preparing to sit down with Michael and discuss his future. It had been a couple of weeks since the incident and they were giving him time to recoup. He had spent the last few nights on the town with Maria.

"He needs therapy."

"He has had therapy, Carly, but I don't think it's going to help. We need a game changer for a while. That detective, what was her name, Alex, she will come for him. I don't know why she dropped her allegations but mark my words, she will come for him and he will mess this up somehow."

Carly didn't know everything; she didn't know the amount of times that Christopher had pulled him back from the brink, or the bodies that lay in the garden behind her. Christopher had been covering for Michael too many times and there was already too much blood on his hands.

"But we know solicitors and judges. I am sure they can have a word with the police."

"It's not a word. Michael is going to get himself into trouble if he doesn't get away from here." Christopher came from behind the desk and sat next to Carly on the sofa.

"It's not forever, baby, just for a while. Take the heat out of the situation. A long holiday if you like, think of it like that. We can send one of the team with him and I don't think we will be able to separate Maria, she will want to go too. A trip around Europe will be good for them both. Harry!"

A large man entered the room dressed in a black suit and tie. Harry Stenson was one of the Mellors' security staff. He was loyal and he knew what Michael was. Harry had helped Christopher with Gary, the star quarterback that was Michael's first kill. And subsequently three other bodies that were lying in the grounds. Harry was also good for threatening a lot of people over the years to not press charges or come back for more money once they had been paid off.

"Get Michael up, will you please?"

Harry just nodded and turned. About five minutes later Michael was in the room, still fully clothed from the night before. "You didn't need to send Harry, you could have just rung."

"I could and you could have just ignored it, it's time, sit down, we need to talk."

"Can I at least have a coffee, a juice or something?"

Christopher nodded to Harry who disappeared to the kitchen.

As Harry walked out Maria walked in, not in the same state as Michael had been, and dressed smartly, hair perfect and with a big smile on her face.

"Morning, Princess."

"Morning, Daddy, Mummy. Michael, they are last night's clothes."

Michael just looked at her and sat down. "Why do I feel I am about to be punished?"

"Not punished, Michael. We just want to talk to you and we need to decide what the next steps are."

"I was attacked, not the other way round." Michael looked directly at his mum with this statement; he knew he couldn't look at his dad. His dad knew what he was.

"Now, Michael, let's just listen to Dad."

Harry placed the drinks on the table and then moved back to the corner of the room.

"Whatever happened in the altercation, Michael, that detective, Alex Keaton? She will come for you. She thinks you're guilty of something and trust me I know a hound dog when I see one."

"But she signed an affidavit."

"I know what she signed, Michael, and I have an idea why she signed it. But nonetheless she is not going to forget that night. My view is you need some distance between you as a cooling off period."

"What distance?"

"A holiday."

"But we have the club to run, don't we, Maria. We can't just get up and leave that."

"We will ensure your club survives, as I am sure that if I am sending you on holiday your sister will want to join you." Maria sat next to Michael on the sofa and held his hand.

"The break will do you good, darling." Carly didn't want to interfere with Christopher's judgement. She didn't know the horrors that Michael had caused but she always felt there was something not quite right with him. A mother's intuition was hardly ever wrong.

"Take the plane, and we have made arrangements in Italy, you leave in three days. Harry has agreed to accompany you for the trip for as long as it needs to be."

"Three days?"

"Three days, Michael, and it is one way. Keep in touch and we will discuss your return. I have been keeping a close watch on Miss Keaton and once we feel this is off her radar you can return."

Michael knew that arguing wasn't going to help his cause. His father had made up his mind and that was that.

"Italy is lovely this time of year. Your father and I spent the whole summer there once, you both love Italy. It will be amazing. "

Michael picked up his orange juice and without saying a word left the room.

"I will look after him, the rest will do us both good." Maria leant over and kissed her mum, then stood up and walked over to her dad and did the same thing, before leaving the room and heading after Michael up the stairs.

"She is a good girl, Carly."

"She is a woman now, Chris, and we can't rely on her to look after Michael all the time, she needs to start to get a life of her own."

"I know, I just hope that she knows it too."

"I love the fact that they are so close, but she needs to find another man in her life other than Michael."

Mother's intuition was kicking in again. The longer that Maria spent with Michael, the less chance that she would make a life for herself away from him. And the less chance for grandchildren.

Chapter 2

Arriving at the church Alex could see Sophie's family greeting people at the door, her mum Sarah and dad Lawrence. Michael was standing alongside them. Paul's parents were too old to make the trip and they were still grieving the loss of their son. She knew that Michael wouldn't miss this. He loved Sophie and over the past six months he had spent nearly every day on the phone to her. Walking up the path Alex could see as all three of them spotted her from a distance. They seemed to be eagerly awaiting her arrival.

"I am so sorry for your loss."

"We are sorry for you too, dear." Sophie's mum hugged her so tight she thought she would lose her breath.

"It's been a hell of a year hasn't it, losing all three in such tragic circumstances."

Sophie's dad wasn't the type to get emotional. He just leaned over and kissed Alex on the cheek and then passed Alex over to Michael.

"Hi."

"Hi, been a while, Alex."

"Yes, sorry, I wish it could have been in better circumstances; I will just go and sit inside."

"No, dear, wait with us, you are as much family as we are, you are all she talked of, you and Paul. I want you to sit with me."

Sophie's mum was persistent. They waited for the last people to enter the church and then they watched as the coffin was taken out of the hearse and up the path. Holding tightly onto Sarah's hand they followed the coffin into the church.

As they walked down the aisle Alex could see Chris standing at the back. He wasn't friends with Paul or Sophie but she had expected him to turn up given their current sleeping arrangements. She didn't acknowledge him as her head was down and at the end of the service he slipped off without anyone announcing that he was there.

Sitting to the right of the church Alex watched as the tears streamed down everyone's faces. The sorrow filled the room but no matter how she tried she couldn't feel the emotion. Sophie was dead and it was the best thing that could have happened to her. Sophie didn't deserve to end up like Mrs McAndrew or Mrs Mesula. And Paul wouldn't have wanted that for his child. Alex's actions were just. At least she believed them to be.

The thought of Paul did bring a welling to her eyes just at the time that Sophie's mother turned to look at her. She was thankful of that.

As they departed the church Sophie's mother grabbed her hand and whispered in her ear. "You are so strong, so strong, I am glad you are here with us."

The coffin was taken into the graveyard where Paul had been buried. Sophie and the little one would be resting with him for the rest of eternity. Michael had asked for that to be put on the headstone. They didn't officially have a name for the child but every day Sophie would call it 'the little one inside me'. Sophie's parents had thought this was a great idea too, so the three of them were acknowledged.

This was where Alex's emotions got the better of her. The tears weren't for Sophie but for the man she had loved. It had been the first time she had visited the grave since the funeral. As they lowered the coffin, each person took a turn to throw a rose into the grave and walked away.

It was a short drive back to the hall where they had prepared a wake for Sophie. With family and some friends attending they laid on food and drink. Alex headed straight for the bar.

"I said I wouldn't ask this today, but do they know anything?"

Alex turned to see Michael standing there. She still couldn't get over how much he looked like Paul and it was making her heart jump just talking to him.

"No, Michael, nothing."

"Mike, Alex – you know I hate Michael. You sound like my grandmother." He smiled at her.

"Sorry, Mike. No nothing, it was just a robbery gone wrong."

"I can't believe that, Alex. Burglars don't want to kill people. What if it was something to do with Paul, to do with the shooting, the mafia?"

"It wasn't, Mike, and we are confident we can rule that out. But as you said it's not for today. How is Sophie's mother doing?" Alex knew she needed to get off topic and soon.

"As well as can be expected, I would say. I don't think it's really hit her yet, her only daughter and her only soon-to-be grandchild lost within weeks of being born."

"She must be devastated."

"She is but Lawrence is a rock, he knows how to say just about enough to care and not enough to upset anyone."

"And you, Mike?"

"I am okay. Can't get over the fact that she is gone though, not so soon after Paul, not so soon after telling us about the baby. Only seems like yesterday they were both over with us on holiday."

"How about your parents, Mike? Did they not want to come?"

"They did, they just didn't think they could manage the journey. It was too far and too soon, they are not young spring chickens any more. And Mum still hasn't gotten over Paul. She said they would make it down to the village church today and pray for us all at the same time. But you know Dad, it will just be an excuse to go over the road for a drink."

"That sounds like a good plan. Come on, let me get you a drink." Mike and Alex moved further towards the bar.

For the next few hours Alex listened to the family remembering their loved and lost ones. Stories of Paul and Sophie were told for the tenth time and everyone had a special memory that they could share. People started to drift and in the end Alex and Mike were the last two standing.

"We should probably go."

"Yes, we should. When are you going back to England?"

"I have a flight tomorrow afternoon, but let's grab some dinner, shall we?"

Alex nodded and fetched their coats from the coat rack in the corner.

"It's not fair, Maria, it's not like I have done something wrong." Maria didn't answer, Michael was in full denial mode. He knew what he had done, but it was always his way of justifying his actions. After each of the altercations happened, they were never discussed again. Except Jack. Jack had been different, Michael considered him the one that got away. And Maria was happy about that. Michael often would use that conversation to try and guilt Maria into letting him do something or go somewhere. If they hadn't have spent so much time upstairs arguing about Jack he wouldn't have left them. It was a small consolation to Maria that he had got away that night, knowing now that he killed himself a few months later.

"It's going to be fun, Michael. Rome, Venice, it's beautiful."

"Yes, but we have the Ox with us, it's not like he is going to let us have fun."

"Harry will be fine, when doesn't he let us do what we want to? Most of the time you forget he is even there."

Michael went over to the table in his room and poured himself a whisky. His room was almost like a mini apartment in the house. There was a bed to one side of the room with a living area opposite. On the wall was a fifty inch TV and a leather sofa that could fit twelve people on comfortably.

"Michael…"

"Don't start, it's their fault I drink, always blaming me for stuff, even getting attacked by someone."

"Dad is just protecting us, Michael. You heard that detective, she blamed you and she didn't seem the forgiving type."

Michael knew deep down this was true. He knew Alex would come for him and in a perverse way it excited him. The thought of being hunted was quite a turn on. "Do you know she is single, and her business partner died in a shooting about half a year ago?"

Maria was taken back a bit by this. "How do you know that, Michael?"

"I have been looking into her, quite the past. Daughter of a cop, sister of a cop. Single, no real relationship to talk of and seems to be married to the job. Spent a while in therapy after the shooting."

"That's dangerous, Michael, don't go and do anything silly. The last thing you need is a policewoman following your every move."

Michael knew what Maria was saying, she didn't need to say it. He had no intention of being caught by Alex. "I won't do anything silly, I was just curious to know who would be coming after me."

Michael sat down on the sofa and Maria came and sat next to him, cuddling up under his arm. "Let's just go to Rome, have some fun and put this all behind us. Just you and me."

Michael drank from the glass as Maria snuggled into him.

Dinner was Italian, Alex was sick of Chinese meals over the past three months and it was good to get out and have a real meal. The conversations kept drifting back to Paul and Sophie but they tried to keep it as fluid as possible. Alex had to remind herself all through dinner that she wasn't with Paul. The similarities were so strong between him and Mike now. When they were together they looked nothing alike but now, it was all she could think of. Not having seen Paul for six months had taken its toll on her. Looking at Mike brought back the feelings she had for Paul, the wine wasn't helping with this either. She had drunk at the funeral but not eaten, so her head had become fuzzy with the alcohol. Her phone had been ringing on and off all day but she had no desire to answer it, not today. Getting through this day was the most important thing. Sophie's parents would go back home and Mike would be back in England tomorrow. She could move forward and get on with her life.

After the meal Alex walked with Mike back to his hotel. It was just around the corner. "It was great to see you, Alex."

"Yeah, you too, have a safe flight and give my love to your parents."

Mike bent down and kissed Alex. It was a little too long and Alex couldn't pull away, the smell of his cologne was the same as Paul's. He looked like Paul. Mike pulled away. There was a moment that they both looked at each other and were thinking the same thing. But Mike made the first break.

"Long day tomorrow."

"Yes. Long day."

Alex walked away, and Mike disappeared into the hotel. As Alex walked her phone bleeped again. Seventeen text messages from Chris, all saying, are you okay, if you need anything call me. I am at home tonight but can come round. There was a call from James also. She didn't want to deal with Chris tonight. So she stood on the corner and rang James.

"You rang?"

"Yes, this is late, everything go okay?"

"Yes, it is all good, and the funeral is done now. Time to move on."

"It was just to say that I was at Jessica Hall's apartment, well crime scene, spoken with all the neighbours and have the names of everyone in the building."

"Okay, can you leave them on my desk for the morning?"

"Already have."

"Thanks, James."

"No problem. See you tomorrow."

Alex hung up, the phone beeped again. This time it wasn't Chris. Alex turned and headed into the hotel. The text had simply said 'Room 314'. Alex knew this wasn't a smart move and she would have to deal with the Chris situation at some point. But she couldn't get that kiss out of her head. She took the elevator up to the third floor, knocked on the door and Mike answered with just his trousers on. They didn't speak, they just embraced and he carried Alex over to the bed. Alex lost herself into him trying not to look him directly in the eye. Every touch, every sensation she felt was from Paul not from Mike. The smell of his

27

aftershave lingered on her lips as she kissed him from head to toe. An hour later and exhausted they both collapsed on the bed.

"I wasn't expecting that."

Alex didn't answer. She was still in the moment and it wasn't Mike she had been with. She had tried to visualise Paul through the whole process, it was him that she really had wanted to sleep with.

The night was short, at five a.m. Alex awoke and left the hotel. Mike was still sleeping and didn't hear her leave. She had gotten good at this over the last few weeks. In the cab on the way home she was reflecting on the events of yesterday; she had had sex with two men in the same day, when up until three weeks ago she hadn't had sex with two different men in the same year. She spent most of the cab ride wondering what was happening to her. She was changing. She just hoped it was for the better.

Alex was home, changed and in the office before seven a.m. The desk sergeant had just started the day shift and there were no more detectives in the building. James had left the list as he promised on her desk and this was a good place to start.

The apartment block where Jessica lived was a small one. She lived at number seven of eleven apartments. It was quite an exclusive part of town. So Alex knew that there was money in the area. Enough to pay for any treatment in, say, Europe for instance. Taking the hard drive out of her drawer she cross matched it against the list that James had left. Surely it wasn't going to be that simple; in fact it was that simple. It jumped out of the page at her.

Oliver Gordon had been visiting his aunt in the building and he was there, there on the list. Oliver Gordon OPM. Obsessive, psychopath, murderous. He was in the building; it was him! Alex was shocked at how simple this was going to be.

Chris walked in the office; he knew she would be in early today having missed yesterday. "Morning."

Alex was taken a bit by surprise as she hadn't seen him walking through the front door. She closed down the PC as quickly as she could.

"Hey." Alex stood up and walked over to him and hugged him. He was surprised by this affection in the work place. This wasn't something Alex had done before. But for Alex it was more out of guilt than anything else. She knew she didn't want to have an awkward conversation with him. And a show of affection would be a good distraction.

"I tried calling."

"I know, I wasn't in the mood for company. I just needed to put my friend to rest."

Chris didn't say anything else. He could see James walking in the building so they parted and Alex went back to the desk.

"Morning."

"James, just in time, let's go over to the Hall apartment block as there is someone I want to meet."

"You have a suspect already?"

"Just a hunch, James, but let's go."

"Coffee first, Alex. Always coffee first."

Chris and James both left the room. Alex went back to her desk and locked the hard drive back in the drawer. James returned with the coffee followed closely by the captain.

"My office, Alex."

James handed her the coffee as she followed him back to the office.

"Sit down. Now I need to discuss Sophie with you."

Alex's heart hit her mouth. He couldn't know anything, nobody could. Why would he want to speak to her about it?

"Okay."

"We should by rights be returning you to desk duty for the next couple of weeks, two traumas in under six months."

"No, Captain, no. I can handle this, I can't handle going back to traffic police."

"Listen."

"Please let me just go back to what I…"

"I said listen and if you had listened you would have heard the words, by rights this is what we should do."

Alex sat back down.

"Now that's better. If you promise one session with the grief counsellor in the next two days you can carry on in the day job."

"Okay, done."

"That was easy."

"Can I go? I have murderers to catch."

"Yes, you can go, but once you have been to see Dr Lee then report back to me, okay, and we can discuss how you are feeling."

Alex was nodding as she left the office and returned to her own.

"Light duties?"

"Nope."

James was secretly hoping for another couple of weeks with his feet up.

"I have to see the counsellor in the next couple of days but other than that we are good to go. Speaking of going, shall we?"

James put his coffee down and grabbed his jacket. Alex was already halfway out of the office. They were out of the building and in the car in less than five minutes.

"Talk to me about Oliver Gordon."

"Oliver Gordon? That's who you suspect?"

"No, not suspect, just an outsider in a regular apartment block, would be the first person of interest I would like to talk to."

"Seems an average type of guy to me, visiting his aunty for two weeks. Said he didn't really know Jessica other than a couple of times he bumped into her in the hallway to say hello."

"What does he look like?"

"Tall, dark hair, a bit like one of those young men on 'The Young and the Restless' now you come to mention it. Why is that important, all killers have a look about them now, do they?"

It's him, Alex thought, I don't know what they do in that lab but when they mix the stuff together these kids come out looking like movie stars. She began to think about Michael again the first time they had met in the club. Everything about him had been intoxicating.

"And, his aunty?"

"Regular aunty I would say, seems a nice woman and they all seemed to love Jessica like a daughter."

Thirty minutes and they were there entering the building. They buzzed to number nine and Mrs Jones let them in.

"I am sorry to bother you, Mrs Jones, we just have a few more questions."

"Come in, dear. Can I get you detectives a drink?"

"Just water will be fine."

James nodded and they stood in the front room whilst Mrs Jones fetched the water.

"Is your nephew still here?"

"I am."

Alex turned to see Oliver standing in the doorway. Six foot four, dark hair, movie style looks even though it appeared as if he hadn't had much sleep. This is definitely our man, thought Alex.

"Please sit, detectives."

Alex and James sat on the couch and Oliver and Mrs Jones sat opposite in two chairs.

"We just have a few more questions." Alex looked down on her pad, there was writing on it. If they had been closer they would have been able to see that it was just a list of things she needed to buy before going home that she had made a few days ago in the office.

"So, Jessica lived directly below you, is that correct?"

"Yes."

"And neither of you heard anything on that night?"

"That's correct, I go to bed around nine and Oliver came in around ten thirty didn't you, dear?"

"Yes."

"When you say came in around ten thirty, where had you been?"

"I was just at the sports bar on the corner; I watched the game and then came home."

"And you spoke with your aunty when you got in?"

"No, dear, Oliver wouldn't wake me, he is a good lad."

He doesn't have an alibi, Alex thought. Oliver looked a little uncomfortable with this.

"I am sure he is, and when was the last time either of you saw Miss Hall?"

"The morning before for me, and Oliver said he did see her in the hallway at lunch time; she often used to come home for lunch. She only worked across the road you know."

Oliver stayed quiet. They had spoken with James yesterday and nothing spooked him but now he was getting nervous. Alex could tell.

"And did you speak to Miss Hall yesterday, Oliver?"

"Briefly, just to say hi."

Alex wrote in her pad: just to say hi – not for any reason other than to make Oliver uncomfortable.

"Okay, that checks out, we just need to take a DNA test from each of you to be able to eliminate you from our enquiries."

James looked directly at Alex; we don't take DNA tests, we don't even know how to.

"DNA tests?"

"Yes, Mrs Jones, we just take a swab of your cheek and then we can match any DNA we find in her apartment or on Miss Hall. We can eliminate you from the suspect list because clearly you have both been in contact with her."

Oliver stood up. Alex's hand went towards her gun but she didn't let anyone see that.

"My partner, James, is going to go to the car to get the kits and we will have this done in less than a minute."

James didn't know what to do, there were no kits in the car. Alex nodded at him and he got up to leave and at the same time Alex got up too. As Alex rose it unsettled Oliver and he jumped straight for the door. Alex's gun was in her hand and pointing at him before he moved three steps.

"Don't."

James was in shock. He turned, pulled his gun and took a step towards the door.

"What is it? What is it?" Mrs Jones started to scream. James went over to Oliver and pushed him against the wall and cuffed him, all the time looking at Alex to see if he was doing the right thing.

"Mrs Jones, Oliver is just going to accompany us to the station for questioning."

"But he hasn't done anything, he was home."

"We will see, Mrs Jones."

James escorted Oliver out of the apartment and placed him in the back of the car as Alex followed out of the building.

"What was that about?"

"He is our man, James, I know he is, that's why I started talking DNA. He may have cleaned up the site but he had sex with Miss Hall and there is no way he could have cleaned inside her and he knows that. Let's get him back to the station and see what he has to say."

It took them forty-five minutes to break Oliver. He had been telling the truth about only seeing Jessica a couple of times in the hallway up until the night of the death.

He had been at the bar and watched the game but so had Jessica. First with some friends but after they left she bumped into him when she was paying the bill. He was charming, handsome, and flirted with her till she stayed for another drink. They then purchased a bottle of wine and went back to her place. Oliver hadn't meant to kill her and it was his first. She had suggested the roleplay and what she wanted him to do. He was a burglar and she was sleeping in bed. As he crept into her room he put his hand over her face and whispered in her ear, 'If you scream you are dead'. He then proceeded to tie her to the bed with the silk scarfs and ripped the clothes off of her. They had strong physical sex.

Mrs Jones had been honest too as nothing was capable of waking her. Not even the sounds of her nephew and Jessica having loud sex underneath her room. After they had both climaxed the excitement had been just too much for Oliver. He grabbed the tie from the curtains and wrapped it around Jessica's throat. At first she laughed but before she knew what was happening it was too late. She had invited him in, set the scene to bring his emotions to the surface and suffered the ultimate price for this.

Oliver Gordon, first degree murder, captured in less than forty-eight hours. Alex was the talk of the station. The captain had called her and James to the office as soon as Oliver had confessed. "Amazing result, Detective."

"Thanks, Captain."

"It was all Alex, Captain, to be fair."

"No, it was both of us, Captain, we went back for further questioning and we could both sense that he was uneasy with the line of questioning."

James didn't reply.

"Either way, good work, it's good to have these things tied up as soon as possible and forty-eight hours I believe is a new record for an empty crime scene case."

"Thanks."

"But Alex, don't think this excludes you from Dr Lee."

Alex knew it was time to get out of there and she and James headed back to their office.

"It was you, Alex."

"It was us, James, if you hadn't have been there we wouldn't have even known to look at him. Don't worry about it. Anyway, gives you more time to look at that suicide."

"Don't you mean us?"

"No, I mean you." Alex smiled and sat back at her desk. She could see a delivery man turn up at the front desk with a bunch of roses. She nodded over to James and then to the desk sergeant and without saying a word implied, who sends roses to a police station? The sergeant in turn nodded back in Alex's direction and a sense of fear washed over her. Were they for her?

"Miss Keaton?"

"Yes."

"For you."

Alex took the flowers and signed the paper. "Are you sure?"

"Yes, Alex Keaton, Care of Station Forty-three. That is you, isn't it?"

Alex sat the flowers on the desk and opened the card as the delivery man left. As he left Chris walked in. She looked directly at him.

"From you?" She wasn't happy to receive flowers, she was a detective whilst she was here, not a woman. James was shocked just at the thought of Chris sending Alex flowers.

"I wouldn't dare."

"Nor would I," said James.

She opened the card, it read: I WILL MISS YOU, M xxx. Mike had sent her flowers to the station. This was awkward with Chris in the same room. She hadn't told Mike anything about Chris as she didn't think there was anything really to say. She hadn't intended to sleep with him; she had managed to get caught up in the moment. And as far as she was concerned she had wanted to sleep with Paul. Alex smiled at both of them.

"I am sure you wouldn't, they are from Sophie's parents for all the support yesterday. That is so sweet of them."

"It did look like a tough day and you did sit with them through the whole thing." Chris was ensuring that Alex knew he was there.

"What do I do with them? Nobody has ever sent me flowers let alone to the office."

James got up and emptied the large glass that was in the corner. "This might hold them."

"Thanks."

Alex left the room and filled the glass with water. She placed the flowers into the glass and put them on her desk. She sat looking at them for about two minutes and then picked them up and put them on the desk in the front office. Came back and sat at her desk once more.

"Better?" James smiled over at her.

'Better' flowers weren't something Alex appreciated. It was a kind gesture but if he had really known her, he wouldn't have sent them.

"So, suicide?"

"Suicide, thinking of that I may as well go and get it over and done with."

"What?" James smiled, as if to imply that she was off to kill herself.

"The shrink, we don't have anything major on, so now is the time."

Alex got up and left the office, heading towards Dr Lee's room down the corridor. One in every three police stations had a resident doctor and the forty-third was that station. Dr Lee had been a resident there for about four years; she had also had a brief encounter with Chris, as most of the women in the building had, even Alex now. She was a tall slender blonde woman, very good looking and very smart. The main reason she wasn't with Chris any more was that she cottoned on to him very quickly.

Alex knocked on the door.

"Come in." Dr Lee was sat at her desk writing. "Alex, I didn't expect to see you so soon, I half expected I was going to need to get the captain to drag you in here by your hair."

Alex smiled at her. Doctors made Alex nervous. Her head was a very private place and she didn't like the thought of someone poking around in there.

"I hear you have had a big win today, congratulations and I would expect exactly what you needed after the events of yesterday and the last few weeks."

It begins, Alex thought. "Yes, lucky, I guess."

"We make our own luck, Alex. Take a seat or if you would rather," Dr Lee nodded towards the couch and smiled at Alex.

"The seat is fine."

"So, been a while? We didn't really finish our last sessions from the shooting incident, did we?"

"No, I think I missed a few appointments."

"You missed most of the appointments, Alex, but I know how hard it is for you to open up so I am not going to push it. You are here now and that is the main thing, so where would you like to start? How are things?"

"Things are good, well not good but you know what I mean. I am doing okay."

Dr Lee sat back in her chair and crossed her legs. "So, in our last session, we were still coming to terms with being unable to sleep, how is that going for you?"

"It's better, the last few weeks in particular, I have been sleeping six to seven hours per night."

"And the drinking?"

"Also better. I still enjoy a glass of wine of a night time but I am no longer buying it by the crate, if you were wondering."

There was a pause in the office. Dr Lee was contemplating her next question. Pushing Alex usually put the defences up so she needed to be careful in how she asked this next question.

"And Paul? Are you still dreaming of him?"

It was Alex's turn to pause, her thoughts went back to last night, back to the hotel room with Mike. She had known it was Mike but in her mind she had slept with Paul, it was his smell, it was his touch, just how she had always imagined it. The kisses were still lingering in her mind. As they did, suddenly the picture of Sophie came into her head. They were walking up the stairs, she could feel herself pulling her gun and then the shot, the blood.

"Alex, I said Paul, are you still dreaming of him?"

Alex brought herself back into reality. "No. No more dreams of Paul. I have moved on," Alex knew as soon as those words were out of her mouth the follow up question was coming.

"Moved on, Alex, is there someone else in your life now? I did see the flowers arrive."

Alex wasn't about to answer questions about her and Chris, especially to one of his old conquests.

"No, I meant that I have moved on, got better, the flowers were a thank you for the help in arranging the funeral and all that."

"Oh okay, and the loss of Sophie, how does that make you feel?"

Alex wanted to say fine, she wanted to say that's why I shot her, she couldn't live any more, not with a baby in her that was designed to kill people, not with a baby who was going to turn into one of the monsters that I hunt down every day. She had to die. That thought lost Alex again. She had to die and I had to kill her – it was my only option. It was the only option.

"Alex?"

39

"Sorry, I was thinking back to yesterday, it was a hard day. And we will find the people that have done this. Losing all three of them in such a short space of time."

"Three, Alex?"

"Yes, three – Sophie was pregnant."

"Sorry, I didn't know, Alex I would like to schedule..."

"The captain said one visit."

"I know he did but I think you still need to talk, Alex."

Alex was already out of the chair.

"I need to get back, Dr Lee, I will think about what you said."

Alex had no intention of returning unless she was ordered to. She didn't need to justify to anyone her actions or her feelings, they were hers. She couldn't share the justification for her actions as nobody else knew about the hard drive. Nobody knew what Jack had uncovered. Dr Smith and the people at the Brown Institute have been playing god with people's lives and this needed careful planning on what to do next. All these people need capturing and Sophie's death doesn't need investigating any further.

Chapter 3

Alex spent the afternoon trawling the internet for murderers. Her laptop was open next to her PC with Jack's list open for all to see. She knew she was safe as James had gone to visit the family of the suicide case. After leaving a note to his family explaining he had been going through some inner turmoil about a girl, the young man had taken a leap off the chaucey bridge. Nothing that was going to interest Alex. She did put his name into the list just to see if something may come of it, but it didn't. What did interest her, though, were all the open cases around the country. Not just country, anywhere in the world she could find an open case on a serial killer she spent time trying to see if she could match someone off the list. Not as easy as she first thought. There was no way to find someone if they weren't mentioned in the report. She had no idea of the people in the area at the time. Although Oliver had been an easy case, it was just a lucky one.

The whole afternoon she was only able to come across one possible suspect. A triple murder case, about three hours' drive from the station. This was outside of the station's jurisdiction zone. Three young women had gone missing over a period of the last six weeks with almost two weeks in between each girl.

They had each been kept alive for at least a week. Raped by multiple men, on multiple occasions, before being strangled and dumped at the road side. It was a small town and there had been no suspects to date.

That's not what piqued Alex's interest though. Whilst she was reading the local newspaper reports on the murders her eye was caught by the celebrations at the local bar. They were celebrating their first year in business and planning a hog roast. It was a small town and she was almost positive that it would have been cancelled figuring what was going on. She checked and it wasn't. The owner of the bar was a guy by the name of Deacon James. Not a local guy, he moved to the area a year ago. After some digging, however, Deacon James was born in France, and by the picture in the paper a dead ringer for James Dean. Alex had a feeling about this, a gorgeous looking man in a town where girls were being killed and raped. Jack's file confirmed it, there in big letters MPOC.

She knew who the murderer was but what could she do about it. Alex couldn't go and arrest him as it was out of her area, and knowing there were protocols to follow for this, she would need a damn good reason. I know who the killer is because I know where he was born wasn't going to be enough.

Alex knew that if he or they hadn't already, they would be taking another girl. With the hog roast tomorrow they had a perfect opportunity.

"Hey."

"Hey."

Alex quickly closed down the laptop as Chris walked into the room.

"How did it go with the doc?"

"You know, she thinks I am crazy and need a holiday."

"Don't we all. Do you want to go and get some dinner together? Looks like we are the last ones here. We can share a car and everything."

Alex didn't want to lose Chris just yet, he had been a welcome distraction over the last two weeks and the thought of going home alone wasn't appealing to her.

"Yeah sure, just give me ten minutes to clear this up."

Chris smiled and left the room. Alex locked the hard drive back in her case and drawer, and then took her phone out. A message from Mike: 'Thanks for a great unexpected night. Take care'.

No kiss? Not very warm considering the flowers. Alex felt it was almost a brush off message. So she just replied: 'Thanks for the flowers'.

Chris came in the office and they headed out to dinner. It was a quiet and sober affair, Alex wasn't really in the mood for chatting and Chris didn't push her, what with the Jessica Hall case, the funeral and a visit to the doctor all within forty-eight hours, he knew she would be tired.

They went back to Alex's apartment. Alex knew how to deal with the situation to keep them to limited talking. She made her move as soon as they were through the door, taking Chris into the bedroom and onto the bed. It wasn't like last night, it was just sex, and Alex made it as believable as possible and once or twice took herself back to Paul as a memory. When they had both climaxed she made no excuses and lay down as if to sleep. Chris cuddled around her as she closed her eyes. She wasn't asleep and she wasn't tired, she just knew that Chris would be.

As she lay there she tried to think of a plan over and over in her mind about Deacon James and what she could do about him. She knew where another killer was and she wanted to catch him and put him out of circulation.

Michael's night was very different, with the intended trip to Italy; his mother had planned a family dinner for the four of them. And as it was her request, he had to attend. Michael and Maria had dressed for dinner and were down in the dining room by nine p.m. They had all been used to eating late, so many parties and functions all started early but you didn't get fed until ten p.m. They were awaiting Christopher's return from his Gentlemen's club where he had been hosting a dinner for a children's charity.

"I thought this was supposed to be a family dinner."

"It is, sweetheart, it's only nine forty-five and your father said he would be here by ten."

"What time is ten p.m. to eat anyway?"

"Given you didn't get up till midday, Michael, I would say it's more like afternoon tea, wouldn't you, Mum?" Maria tried to keep Michael in check; he was still acting out from this morning's news.

As the limo swung into the driveway, Michael headed for the drinks cabinet and then went and sat at the dining room table like a petulant child.

Christopher came through the front door and they all headed for the table.

"Sorry I am late, the presentations went on a little."

"That's okay, Dad, we weren't doing anything. And I am sure the awards were more important."

"You weren't doing anything," Michael snapped back. But nobody acknowledged his response. The staff began to serve dinner to them all.

"How was your day, Maria?"

"Nothing special, played tennis, caught up with a bit of my correspondence, I helped Mum with the charity which was really nice. We have planned quite a few fundraisers for later in the year."

There was a silence at the table. Christopher was looking at Michael who was sitting staring at his glass.

"Michael? And how about you?"

"I wasn't attacked again, Father, if that is what you are asking?"

Christopher just returned to his dinner, he didn't want to make a scene. Michael knew what he was, Michael knew that his father and his sister both knew what he was, but when he was in front of his mother he became a child.

"Carly?"

"It was a good day, my dear. Maria was a star as always."

"I hadn't finished, Father."

"Oh, you hadn't? I just presumed that you had stayed in your room all day with a bottle of whisky and a big pouting lip."

Michael rose from the table and before he could get a word out, Christopher shouted at him.

"Sit down! You want to act like a child, Michael, I will start to treat you like one."

Christopher turned to Harry as he was standing in the corner of the room, almost as invisible as the furniture. "Harry, make the arrangements as he goes to Italy tomorrow evening. You can have the day to pack. This needs to stop. You come back when you are a grown up"

Michael slammed down his plate and exited the room.

"You don't need to go with him, dear, you do know that. Harry will look after him, won't he Christopher?" Christopher nodded at Carly.

"I know but I want to. I will help him, you will see, and when we come back he will be a totally new man."

"Here is hoping, dear."

The rest of the meal was eaten almost in silence. Christopher felt guilty knowing what he was sending Maria into, but he also knew if anyone had a chance of changing Michael it was going to be her.

Alex woke as Chris was in the shower. She went and made the coffee and brought it back to bed.

"Hey that's my job."

"I know, I was up, so I thought I would make it." Chris went over and kissed her on the head. He placed his coffee on the table and started to get ready.

"Are you coming in?"

"Do you know, I think I am going to take a long weekend. Dr Lee recommended I do and so did the captain."

"Sounds like a plan, we can stay in bed all day if you like?"

"I was kind of thinking that I would have a me day, just some time to myself to process everything that has gone on, maybe tidy this place and get a haircut, shave my legs, all those things you can't do when you spend most of your time in bed, at home."

Chris smiled at her. "I think it will do you good, maybe dinner tonight?"

"Yes, maybe."

Chris grabbed the rest of his coffee, kissed her again and left, leaving Alex alone in the apartment. This had been the first time Alex had been alone for a while. Chris had been a welcome distraction over the past few weeks but this was now getting in the way of what was coming. She liked Chris but he wasn't boyfriend material. Alex got the feeling that this wasn't how Chris was starting to feel. Chris had not said the words yet but she felt like they were coming. She had seen a different side of him now, a caring considerate side and at any other time in her life she would have welcomed this with open arms but not today. Not at this moment in her life.

Alex got up and tidied the front room and the kitchen area which took all of forty-five minutes. This wasn't the real reason that she wanted to take a personal day from work. She had decided to take the three hour drive to see Deacon James. If they hadn't already, they were about to take another girl. With a two day hog roast starting today to celebrate the first anniversary of their opening of the bar, she knew this would be a perfect opportunity for them, and she wanted to be there to stop it.

After showering she made the bed and finished tidying as much as possible. She packed a small bag; if she couldn't make anything happen today then she was determined to stay over into day two. The drive went quicker than expected. Alex took the time to play over and over in her head what she was going to do with the hard drive. Should she own up to it, would they believe her if she did? Also, was it going to make her a suspect in Sophie's murder? Because Sophie's baby was on the list and if she came clean they would know Alex had the knowledge for a while. They would certainly ask Dee when she handed the information over, and the longer she let it go on the more she was going to look guilty. She was part of this list now and she couldn't risk the fact that they may start looking at her. Jack's discovery had made her into a murderer and whilst that was against everything in her moral code, she couldn't truly tell herself she wouldn't do the same thing again.

Driving through the town she could see there were fewer than five hundred houses. How was the party still on if three of these houses had lost daughters?

The bar, named Deacons, was just off the side of the road; a few cars were parked out front and about five motorcycles. As she got out of the car she could hear music and conversation so she presumed there must have been a garden out back. Checking her gun was at her side she went into the bar.

It was a typical biker's bar, it was centred to the middle of the room with a pool table on one side. The back doors were open leading to the garden where she could see a number of people standing talking.

"Can I help you?" It was Deacon, Alex recognised him from the picture in the paper, and he was even better looking in real life.

"Just a Bud, please." With that he stepped away and brought back a bottle.

"Not local?"

"No, just visiting a friend and she told me you were having a party so I thought I would come and check it out."

"Well, you are more than welcome, the hog is on and we will be eating soon." With that he disappeared to the end of the bar.

Alex couldn't get over his striking features, much like Michael, Stephen, even Joseph Manning the lawyer she met up town. They were all so model-like. Alex never knew but Deacon's father had served with Joseph Manning's father in the army. That's how he was born. He was another recommendation to the Brown Institute. Alex had stumbled into a pocket of Brown Institute children. Due to the nature of the procedure and the cost and the confidentiality it was soon clear to the Brown Institute that people talk. And these families generally kept close. It had been something that Dr Jonathan Smith had been looking into in his files, back in Germany.

Alex wandered out to the garden. There were about forty people out there, some tables and chairs and, as Deacon had explained, a hog roasting across an open fire. All the time she wandered around, she could see Deacon looking at her out of the corner of his eye. She had made the desired impact. She had dressed herself to become the honey trap. Well, as much as she could, she hadn't had a lot of experience in this matter. In fact, the last time that she wore this much makeup was the night of playing the part of a hooker to catch a murderer in the park. The first night she had kissed Chris. It seemed like a long time ago to Alex now.

If Deacon and his little gang of rapists were going to attempt to take anyone she wanted it to be her.

Alex sat watching the dynamics of the bar over the next couple of hours, keeping herself to herself. She had purposely been to the bar half a dozen times for a beer and then secretly tipped most of it away into the garden when nobody was looking. She wanted to appear vulnerable.

Deacon rarely left the bar, other than to take the first slice of the hog. At the bar two other guys were close to him at all times.

A large red headed gentleman by the name of Alastair, about six foot, looked like he could have been a lumberjack or some kind of tradesman. And another big guy simply called Huck. Huck hardly spoke, it was Deacon and Alastair doing all the talking. They were his partners in this little venture she was sure of it. There was no shortage of young girls in the bar though. Even given what had been going on over the last six weeks. Alex knew this was Deacon's doing. Moths to the flame, but she was a little older, a little more experienced and made the point on several occasions that she was just passing through. Nobody was going to miss her.

Chris had sent her several texts during the day, checking up on her to see if she was okay and okay for dinner. She didn't reply. She didn't want him involved in this.

As the day turned to night they had all moved back into the bar. The hog had been mostly eaten and the remains of it were put out on trays at the bar. It was going to be harder to hide her drink in here. But she had drunk at least ten bottles, or so they thought.

"Another?"

"Why not."

"My name is Deacon by the way," as he held his hand out.

"Sophie." As soon as the words left her lips she felt guilt for the first time. Not guilt about the shooting but guilt that she was about to use her best friend's wife's name to catch a murderer.

"Pleased to meet you, Sophie. I hope you are not driving?"

"No, I was going to just check into the motel up the road, my friend says they always have rooms so I will do it when I leave."

Alex had not only planted in their heads she was a stranger, but she was a stranger that nobody was expecting tonight.

Her phone went off in her pocket again. It was a text message from Mike which just read: 'Flowers?' with a smiley face at the end. This was more of the flirtatious Mike she had known from her visit to England.

She did reply to this, just as a distraction from the bar and the fact that she had been ignoring her phone most of the day. She just replied: 'Yes, thank you'.

"Boyfriend, Sophie?" Deacon was back in front of her at the bar.

"No. He wishes though, sometimes you can just never get far enough away from them, can you."

Deacon poured a shot on the bar for both him and Alex. "Here is to men, may they never darken your door again."

"Well, I didn't say all men." Although it had been a long time since Alex had to flirt even she knew that was a pick up line.

Deacon smiled and went back to the end of the bar where Alastair and Huck had been sitting, drinking all day. Alex knew they had her firmly in their sights. She watched as the bar got quieter and quieter and continued to order Buds, walking around the bar and dropping them on the tables where there were already a lot of empty bottles and glasses, sometimes taking the bottle into the toilet with her so she could empty it and refill it with water. This was a dangerous game she was playing as, through this, she had actually been drinking a little.

She sat at the bar with only the last few people remaining and Deacon and his crew pretending to watch a rerun of a baseball game on the TV when her phone rang. Withheld number. This wouldn't be something she would normally answer but she had a full bottle in front of her and it would give her an excuse to walk around.

"Hello?"

"Hello, Detective, did you like the flowers?"

"Mike."

"I am not sure we are at the Mike stage yet, Alex, last time we met you were convinced I was Michael, Michael the murdering psychopath with a silver spoon in his mouth."

Alex felt a cold shiver down her back. Michael – the flowers had been from Michael Mellor, that's what the M stood for.

"Michael, how did you get this number?"

"I have my ways, Detective. Anyway, I thought I would just let you know that I will miss you as I have decided to take a little trip, a trip somewhere where few people will know me and I can have some fun. You know fun, Detective, the kind of fun I was having with that young man before you rudely interrupted our night."

"I saved him."

"He wasn't yours to save, Alex, he was mine." Michael's voice sounded so much like his father's at that point, full of authority.

"I will get you, Michael. You will pay for all the things you have done."

"Alex, no need for all that, besides you have no idea what I have done and what I am capable of doing."

"Michael."

"Sorry have to go, we're about to taxi, do hope to see you soon." With that Michael put the phone down.

Michael was sitting on the plane as Maria walked out of the toilet. "Who was on the phone?"

"It was just Jane from the club, another busy night and everything was fine."

"Good." Maria sat opposite him and poured him a glass of champagne.

"To new beginnings, Michael, let's leave the past in the past?"

"I couldn't agree more."

Chapter 4

Alex had wandered out of the bar into the front car park. She was trying to work out in her head what had just happened. Michael was almost taunting her to come and get him. She couldn't get the picture of that young man out of her head as he lay on the floor covered in blood. She could see herself projected into that position. She emptied her bottle and headed back into the bar, trying to regain focus as she did.

"Another drink, Sophie?"

"Yes, please."

"Still the boyfriend, sorry want-to-be boyfriend?"

"Yes, still him, but he knows his place now. I have told him to stop calling and give me some space." Alex needed a minute; in the time that she had been on the phone the bar had cleared other than the three of them. Whatever was coming was coming soon.

She got up taking her drink to the toilet with her and closed the door behind her. She went to the wash basin and washed her face until she was alert, all the time thinking through her head, Michael is going to have fun. She knew a murderer was out there and about to take his rage out on someone. But she also knew three more murderers were outside her door waiting for her. She emptied her bottle and filled it with cold water. Undoing the clip on her gun she returned to the bar.

Alastair and Huck had moved to the middle of the bar, close to where she had been sitting.

"What has happened to everyone? Not much of a party if everyone keeps going home, is it?"

Alastair and Huck turned and smiled at her. She took her bottle of water and drank it down in one. "Seems like we will be drinking alone, gentlemen."

Alex went back to the bar where Deacon was just taking the top off another bottle of beer. As he smiled at her, for a second she saw Michael's face looking back at her with the intent of murder in his eyes. She shook it off just in time to see something drop into the bottle, drugs Alex thought, rohipnol something like that, this is their move.

As he passed the bottle to Alex she knocked it onto the floor as if by accident. "Oops sorry, didn't mean to do that."

"No problem, I will get you another." Deacon turned his back this time, to drop in the pill. Alex already knew what was going on, Alastair and Huck had moved behind her as if to pretend to play pool.

"There's no harm, no foul." Alex took the drink and set it on the bar.

Deacon stood in front of Alex as if waiting for her to take a sip.

"You know, maybe I should go or at least have some water." Alex knew those words were going to spark a reaction; before the sentence was finished Deacon had grabbed her arm.

"Not likely." Alastair and Huck were behind her, they weren't doing anything as Alex was only tiny. They had no doubt that Deacon was going to handle this but they were wrong.

Alex drew her weapon and without losing contact with Deacon, turned and fired two shots, one shattering Alastair's knee and another in Huck's arm. Both men fell to the ground in screams of pain. Before Deacon knew it the gun was under his chin.

"I know what you are, Deacon James, and I know what you have been doing."

"If you knew you would have never come in here, little girl."

Deacon head-butted Alex and knocked her backwards onto the floor where Alastair and Huck were. Her eyes were full of water and it hurt like she had been hit by a baseball bat. She could smell the blood again, just as she had in the Marriott hotel when Paul was shot, but this time it was her blood as her nose began to bleed. Adrenaline started to go through her veins, it was kill or be killed. She could see Deacon heading to the end of the bar. Reaching for her gun, someone grabbed at her arm. It was Alastair. She managed to reach it and dispatched a bullet straight between his eyes. Huck was moving but not closer to Alex, further away, he was heading for the door. Alex managed to turn and get one in his leg. He buckled and hit the floor. Deacon was all over her, he hit her across the cheek with a full blow that nearly took her head off; any other day that would have sparked Alex clean out, but not today. She knew if it did she would not be waking up again. The gun that had come out of her hand was lying two feet away again. She managed to reach it with her leg and flick it back towards her hand. As Deacon bore down for another go Alex pulled the gun and shot him twice in the shoulder knocking him backwards against the bar. Alex composed herself. She kept an eye on Huck in the corner, he was rolling around on the floor screaming in pain and then she got up and stood over Deacon.

"How many?" Alex screamed at him. "How many?"

"How many what?"

"How many women, how many women have there been in your short pathetic life? How many daughters are there buried in the ground or by the side of a road somewhere?"

"I don't know what you mean."

Alex knelt in front of him, not close enough for a head-butt as she had learned that lesson, but close enough to look him square in the eye. "One chance, you tell me the number and I will let you live."

Deacon sat there in silence.

"The number for your life, it is as simple as that."

Deacon still sat there, but now he was weighing his options. Alastair was dead. Huck was shot twice and for a big man wasn't going to come and take this little woman on.

"Twenty-six."

Alex was shocked at the number, it almost threw her backwards. This man had raped and murdered twenty-six women and she was about to become twenty-seven.

She stood up contemplating her next move. Twenty-six was enough. It took one shot straight through his head and into the bar behind Deacon was never going to reach twenty-seven.

Alex walked over to Huck; he was already cowering in the corner. "How many?"

"What, I have nothing to do with this, I was just playing pool."

"How many?"

"I didn't do anything, I didn't, I have never killed anyone."

Suddenly Alex had that thought, what if he and Alastair hadn't killed anyone. There were traces of rape from multiple men in these girls but it's not to say that they all had a hand in the murder. Was rape enough to kill someone over?

"I didn't kill anyone, the last girl, Stacey something. Stacey, I did hurt her, I did, we all did but when we left the bar she was still alive. She was with Deacon." Alex had been trying to compose herself quickly, two dead, need a witness. The words stuck in her head, when we left the bar she was alive. From the reports she read she believed that they had been kept alive a week.

She looked down at Huck. "So just a rapist?"

Huck didn't reply and just nodded. Without thinking Alex shot him, it wasn't intended to be a fatal shot but there was going to be no way he would have the equipment to rape anyone ever again. The bar was silent other than the groaning of Huck on the floor. Alex sat on the stool and tried to compose her thoughts.

"You know, Huck, what went down here tonight is all your fault, if you hadn't hurt Stacey then this wouldn't have happened to any of you."

"Fuck you."

"Not something you would be able to do now is that, Huck."

Alex felt a rush. There was an intoxication around what had happened here. It was the same feeling she had after leaving Sophie's, as if she had been doing the right thing. She was thinking back to Oliver Gordon and how she had wished that the situation had got out of hand. There was a real kind of justice in what she was doing – it was almost biblical.

She picked up her phone, there was a text from a withheld number which simply read: 'Italy is lovely this time of year x'.

Michael, yes Michael, you are on my list. Alex sat and thought for a minute. List, list, there is no Stacey missing on that list. The three women that had been taken from the town were Mary Jane, Jane, and Sue Ellen. She remembered as it seemed like an episode of 'Little House on the Prairie'.

Alex quickly got up and headed over to Huck.

"You said Stacey, Stacey who?"

"Fuck you."

"Huck, I am serious. Stacey who, and now! Or you are going to end up like your friends."

"Just Stacey, I don't know her last name, last night when we were in the bar."

I was too late, Alex thought, they had already taken someone. Alex had done such a good job all day it made them change their pattern, she was alone and vulnerable, drunk and with nobody looking for her. Deacon couldn't miss the opportunity.

Alex knew there was a chance that Stacey was still here. Deacon liked to play with them for a while before killing them. She drew her gun again; although she was convinced that there was nobody else there, she didn't want to take the chance. In the corner there was a door to the cellar and a door to the upstairs. Alex just kept thinking, where would you keep her, Deacon?

Alex chose the door to the cellar and slowly went down the steps. It was pitch black, she could just about make out a pull switch in front of her and so she pulled it. The lights came on; there were barrels of beer and bottles of liquor stacked in the corners of the room and in the middle of the room a body with a sheet lay across it. Had Deacon changed his habits and killed her sooner because of what she had done today? This was guilt. Alex walked closer to the sheet and pulled it back. A young man in his twenties was underneath. It seemed like he had been hit around the head with a baseball bat or something just as heavy as half of his head had been smashed in. John Beresford had been the third member of Deacon's gang until Sue Ellen. Guilt had got the better of him and he was threatening to go to the police. Deacon didn't take care of it himself; he made Alastair do it, so that he knew he had something on Alastair going forward. Alex was relieved that it wasn't Stacey; she left the basement and took the second door to the upstairs.

At the top of the stairs she walked into an open-plan room. It was certain no entertaining was ever done here. There was a couch, a TV and a mattress on the floor in the corner. Deacon didn't keep possessions so as to enable a quick getaway.

On the mattress she could see Stacey still alive. Bound, gagged and blindfolded. Alex put her gun away and went over to her, took her blindfold off and untied her. She picked up the phone at this point and dialled 911. There was still a long night ahead.

By the time the backup and ambulance had arrived Alex had Stacey downstairs and out of the front door. She had been beaten black and blue and raped a number of times but at least she was still alive. More than could have been said for Huck; he was dead before the ambulance arrived. When Alex had shot him she managed to hit an artery and he bled out whilst Alex was sitting with Stacey.

Alex explained to the police sergeant who she was, that she was just passing and then was attacked by these guys. They had bragged about what they were going to do with her and what they had done in the past and she had somehow managed to get free from them. The police sergeant was delighted with the story and the fact that she had helped them to capture the culprits. Capture had been his words even though Alex knew no one was still alive. Alex was just keen to get home. They offered her a place for the night but she declined and made her excuses to leave, ensuring they knew if they needed more they could contact her tomorrow or in the office on Monday.

Alex drove the three hours home and went straight into the shower. The journey home smelt of blood, she smelt of blood and she needed to get rid of it. As she stood in the shower she played the events of the night over and over again in her head, realising that she was in danger from the moment she had walked into the bar. If she hadn't noticed the pill, if she hadn't been distracted by the other known murderer phoning her, if she hadn't got off the early shots to Alastair and Huck, she would have been dead now or worse, tied next to Stacey for a week before they got bored of her and killed her too. She stayed in the shower until it started to run cold. Alex collapsed on the bed and slept. It was eight hours straight through without the hint of a dream. The only thing that woke her was the postman knocking the door at eleven a.m.

Chapter 5

Michael and Maria's plane landed in Italy in the early hours of Saturday morning. The limo had been waiting to take them to the apartment their parents had bought close to the Vatican. It was a small modest penthouse apartment by their standards, not like the villas they had all over the world, but it was quaint. Within a five minute walk there were a few coffee shops, bars and restaurants. It was all good quality Italian food and very authentic. Carly had fallen in love with the place every time she visited. It was only a twenty-five minute walk into the centre of Rome which was just the right distance for a stroll in the sunshine.

Michael hated it, it wasn't modern. There was no TV but his father had insisted they stay there. Michael didn't need distractions and this was the most tranquil place he knew to send him. Tranquil, and not covered with girls or boys with a lack of clothing. Christopher was keen to take temptation away from Michael. With Harry never more than twenty feet away Michael was not going to get a choice of where he stayed and how to behave.

They both slept most of the morning away, a mixture of jet lag and the amount of champagne they drank on the plane.

"Michael, come on, get up so we can go for a walk."

"Walk to where?"

"I don't know but if we head towards town we will pass the Pantheon on the way and that little Irish bar on the corner you like.

The Scholars Lounge or something like that? Then maybe do some shopping."

Michael reluctantly got out of bed and went into the living room. Harry had arranged for coffee and bagels to be delivered, which neither of them thanked him for. It was to be expected that they couldn't look after themselves.

"It's about half an hour from here."

"Michael, look outside, it's gorgeous and we are in one of the most gorgeous cities in the world. Let's have some quality time here."

Michael carried on eating his bagel and drinking his coffee.

"Besides, there are some art exhibitions opening and we need to ensure we get some tickets for the week."

"We have the thing at the Vatican tonight, don't we? The one Mum set us up for? And then we can just send Ox to get the rest, can't we?" Harry didn't move.

"No! And don't call Harry Ox, Michael. I don't know what we would do without him." Harry still didn't move, standing still and not reacting to Michael had become quite an art form over the last few years.

"Besides it will be good to get some time in the sun, it's been far too long, Michael."

Michael didn't want to upset Maria. She was his only true friend in the world. There had been others, groupies mainly that would stick around with the both of them. But generally that was to increase status or to try and get some of their money.

Michael finished his breakfast and got dressed. "Come on then, Sis, let's take a walk, but keep the shopping down to a minimum, agreed?"

"Agreed."

Maria loved it when Michael was being loving; there was no indication of the terror she knew that lay inside him. He was her loving brother. It was a twenty minute walk to the Pantheon. Michael had said it was too crowded to go in, so they sat at the fountain just outside. Maria had picked up a couple of ice creams and they sat watching the people go in and out. Harry was sitting in the coffee shop to the right of the building watching closely.

"Do you know it was built before Christ, well the first time?"

"I know it was built a long time ago." Michael wasn't a believer; his parents had made him go to church the same as Maria but it didn't excite him like it did her. He didn't want to upset her, so he used to play it down a lot.

Maria didn't look for a response.

"Raphael is in there, so is Carracci and Corelli."

"Corelli – didn't he like to play mandolin or something? I am sure I have seen a film somewhere."

Michael was smiling at Maria, as they sat eating their ice creams. He was also smiling at the bunch of lads who were taking pictures of each other in the front of the building, all young Swedish or Dutch looking types who looked like they could be descended from Vikings.

"Stop taking the mickey, Mickey. Also some of the bronze they melted off the roof four hundred years ago is also in St Peter's Basilica, and in Castel Sant'Angelo. That's not far from here, can we see that?"

"Yes, sure we can."

"Madonna del Sasso was made by Lorenzetto, based on Madonna, after her song 'Material Girl'."

"That's good."

"You are not even listening to me, Michael." Maria punched him on the arm. "This is our holiday time for me and you." Michael recoiledbackwards and smiled.

"Sorry, you are right, plenty of time for other stuff. How about we take a wander down there to the little Irish bar and then to Centro Storico and then shopping."

"Sounds perfect."

Michael took one last look over at the young men as he got up to leave. Maria noticed him looking and quickly linked arms with her brother.

"We can go to the Coliseum if you like?"

"Not today, you know it's my favourite; I am going to save it. Rome wasn't visited in a day you know." Maria was glad all his attention was back on her.

Alex put her dressing gown on and went to the door. The postman handed over a small box the size you would keep trainers or shoes in. She signed for it and placed it on the side in the kitchen. Thoughts started to go through her head; she didn't get deliveries, flowers a few days ago and now this. This was from Michael, she was convinced of it. After last night's call and the text message she was quickly ruling out a bomb or a snake in the box. He wanted to play with her. Nonetheless she still took a knife to the box and opened it very carefully. When the lid came off there was a small statue of the Coliseum in the box, a note saying 'Monday eight p.m.' and a first class return ticket to Rome, taxi to and from the airport and hotel accommodation within a ten minute walk.

Did he honestly believe she was going to fall for this? She knew if he was taking her to Rome he wouldn't intend to let her come back.

Michael was seeing how many buttons he could push on Alex. Her phone rang at the same time; she went into the bedroom and lay on the bed preparing a conversation with Michael in her head as she did.

"Hi."

"Hi." It wasn't Michael, which surprisingly was a little disappointing.

"I rang yesterday?" Chris had started to feel distant from her, two nights out of the last sixteen they had been apart and they were almost in succession.

"I know I am sorry, things got away from me."

"So what are you doing with your days off? Want to do something together?"

Alex hadn't given it a second thought, well she hadn't given Chris a second thought, her only thought over the last twenty-four hours was to see how many people she could cross off Jack's list. He had given her the keys to the door and she was adamant this wasn't going to be wasted.

"I am going to visit my parents today."

"Oh okay, tomorrow?"

Alex paused, he wasn't going to give in, and she didn't want to lose him at the moment or start giving him reasons to suspect her of anything. He was the M.E. and the IT guru in the station but he was fast turning into a good detective.

"Do you want to come join me?"

"Join you?"

"At my parents' tomorrow for dinner? My dad always cooks on Sundays, it's the only time he does. And he always cooks way too much."

"I would love to." Chris's head started to fill with confidence; he hadn't expected to meet her parents so soon. Well not formally anyway, he had met her dad and brother at the station but that was in line with work. Alex had the reaction she wanted.

"It's a date then, come around about two p.m. I will text you the address."

"Okay, looking forward to it." Alex sensed a pause. Chris was about to say something that she didn't want to hear, it felt like three little words or at least a conversation leading towards them.

"Bye." Alex hung up the phone.

She had bought herself the day with that offer, which means she could start work on what was really important. But to do that she needed to get into the office and get the hard drive.

Within two hours she was sitting back in her apartment. She had phoned her parents on the journey over to the station and explained that they were coming to dinner and they were delighted, her brother would be there too so it would be a big family meal. Her dad had been really excited about the prospect of that. It had been far too long since the last one. Not really what Alex wanted but it would provide a nice distraction.

Alex sat at the computer in the living room and uploaded the hard drive. She needed a plan to start to capture these people, something that wasn't going to make her stand out. But there was no way of tracking them down. From the age of eighteen no more records were filled in, They had become adults. Their last known address from that point was that of their parents. Some of these people were reaching forty now.

Alex went over to the kitchen and pulled out Jack's letter that he had given to his father. The code was where it needed to start.

P = Psychopath

O = Obsessive

M = Murderous

C = Compassionate

L = Loyal

OC = Obsessive compulsive

She needed to sort the list by P&M and then cross reference all last known addresses and unopened cases. Or cross the names off the list. That was going to be a quicker way; if they were already locked up then she could eliminate them.

Alex sat and reread the letter, she almost missed Jack. He had started all this and still they never met. Well, not when he was alive anyway. He would have been the only person who would understand what she was trying to do. Her mind started to wander to Jack's wife Dee. From the tape and her time with Dee, she believed there was a love between them that Alex was sure she was never going to experience. He had loved her totally and lost his way, whilst she still loved him despite his faults.

Alex sat staring at the computer. She sorted all the P&Ms into a separate file and included date of birth and last known destinations. There were medical conditions and check-up data on the files also but this wasn't going to be relevant to her search.

Antonio Anisia was the name at the top of the list. An Italian. Alex ignored the obvious signal there and the desire to grab the ticket out of the box and go looking for him. She opened her laptop and dialled into the police mainframe. Nothing. He wasn't in America. They had little access to the Interpol files other than confirmation of a conviction. There was one but he had been released six months ago. Antonio Anisia had spent seven years in prison for manslaughter. It was a fight in a bar in Milan. Few eye witnesses could confirm who actually started it, and as he was outnumbered three to one the judge believed his plea that he didn't start it.

Alex went onto the internet and typed in his name. As soon as the picture came up from his social media page, she believed he started the fight. He was shirtless in the photo and could have been one of the statues out of the museums.

Alex would have been right in predicting this. Antonio had spent most of his life getting into scrapes, but this time was different. These three guys, Vincent, Olivier and Giorgio had been terrorising the local community for years. They always took what they wanted when they wanted. They had left a number of people with broken bones and beaten faces but never been reported.

Vincent's father was high up in government and people were afraid of him. The rumours were rife that he had a connection into the Mafia as did Olivier's father. Giorgio was just there to tag along with them.

Antonio had gone looking for trouble that night. He knew the coffee shop that they sat at every Friday and Saturday night, everyone did. He knew if he sat in their booth then there would be repercussions. When he walked into the coffee shop and the owner came round to serve him, asking if he would prefer another seat, Antonio had declined.

Within thirty minutes Vincent's little gang had entered and were standing over Antonio. He was ready for them, as the first punch came towards him he blocked the hand, held it to the table and stabbed a knife off the table straight through his hand.

Antonio took a couple of blows to the head before another knife off the table took Vincent in the leg. Vincent dropped the knife he was carrying and Giorgio picked it up.

Antonio managed to go backwards and get out of the booth and as Giorgio swung the knife at him, Antonio turned it round and plunged it into Giorgio's chest. He bled out on the floor. The other two ended with minor injuries to the hand and the leg and a few bruises from Antonio's right hook but nothing serious. The sight of the blood pooling across the floor had stopped Antonio as he fixated on it.

Vincent's father had demanded justice for all three. The shop's owner didn't say anything out of fear, but it had been the tourists in the corner that had given statements to the police stating that Vincent started this. The most Vincent's father could pressurise the judge into was to charge him with manslaughter and a sentence of seven years.

Alex typed in Vincent Lorenzo into the internet. As the first word appeared Alex knew they weren't going to be in need of her help. Vincent was missing and so was Olivier. Antonio had been released and within three months both of his opponents had been taken care of and now he was in the wind. With the whole of the police force in Milan and potentially half the Mafia there was no point in Alex joining in this investigation.

After a while Alex stood up and poured herself a glass of wine. She was still feeling the bruises from last night and her head had started to hurt. She had spent the last couple of hours trying to sort the list and looking up murderers but this was frustrating, there was no easy way of doing this.

Over the next few hours she continued to research, barely touching the top ten A's on the list. Two were already in prison and the bulk of them were across Europe. This wasn't a surprise given that the Brown Institute had been based in Paris. This wasn't going to help her and all she could think of was that she would be better placed in Europe to catch these people.

Getting up and moving away was not an option. Her family were there and she needed them. Alex felt herself slipping back into the old

Alex, the one who drank too much every night and missed sleep through the tears. Not having Chris there meant there was nobody to regulate what she had been drinking, and before she knew it she was two bottles down and was opening the third. The laptop was closed and she lay in silence thinking about Jack, the case, the Institute, what these people had been doing to the world and how that made her feel. Jack was one of them and when he found out, he took care of himself with a shotgun. But Alex didn't know how many others knew where they came from, and should they? If you tell someone they are a murderer does it make them one? Alex was becoming obsessed with the whole, do I? Don't I? scenario but neither of those solutions ended well. She had the knowledge and it should only be her to deal with this, but at some point she was going to have to stop the flow. This experiment was still going on, in Germany now. Alex could see Dr Smith's face in her mind when she asked him about the letters, and there was a mixture of fear and accomplishment at the same time. He knew what he was doing and Alex knew at some point he was going to have to pay for his crimes.

The third bottle wasn't finished before she passed out on the sofa.

Chapter 6

Michael and Maria arrived at the Vatican Museum. There were no queues outside, the museum had been closed since six p.m. and it was a private arrangement tonight in aid of charity. It had been almost $250,000 per ticket for a private walk through and a drinks reception in the Sistine Chapel. Carly had set it up for them as they all loved walking through there as a family when they were little. As they entered the foyer they were each handed a set of earphones if they wanted to listen to the guide. They didn't; this wasn't their first visit. It was their tenth. Maria loved the art and the sculptures, religion had been a big part of her life and she knew just as much as the tour guide did. Michael knew that he would be listening to his sister's commentary on the way round.

Michael had an underlining conflict with the museum. He didn't believe in God, but there was something dark about this place. He believed if you looked closely enough at all the paintings and the sculptures they were more evil than good. For every one picture of a saint holding a baby there were three of a soldier killing one. The sculptures were mainly of men, with naked men, in the pictures too there was something primevil in the House of God and it would always get Michael's blood boiling. Babies battling a crocodile, the assassination of Julius Caesar. All of these Michael would watch through his own eyes, whilst half listening to Maria on the way around.

The sculptures at the beginning of the tour disappeared and turned into tapestries, every second one with Jesus emerging to all-out anarchy going on around him. The hundreds, thousands of hours spent creating these pictures, Michael couldn't decide if it was for good or for evil. Maria knew the Vatican Museum had this effect on him; it had been getting steadily worse every time they came so she didn't hang around. Before they knew it they were in the hall of maps. The gold ceiling had a calming effect on Michael and the maps were just showing the unification of Rome. She purposely spent a while in this hall delaying the move into the Sistine Chapel as she knew Michael had problems with the art in there also.

Whilst most people remark on the hand of God in the centre of the ceiling Michael had become obsessed with Michelangelo's 'Last Judgement' behind the altar. He would always comment on the bloodshed needed to get to heaven, the fighting, and the empty skin of Michelangelo himself in the painting. All men, always men, for Michael it was as if God had been justifying who he had become and how he was feeling. Maria was keen to not have that type of holiday.

As they entered the Sistine Chapel there was rope at every wall so you could not get close to the tapestries hanging there. And just down the steps in the middle of the room was a table with champagne and hors d'oeuvres laid out.

"Michael, are you listening to me?" He wasn't, he was already looking at the picture.

"Sorry, Sis."

"I said it took four years to paint this room, and he hated doing it. If it wasn't for the pope he would have never even started. How does it go again – 'since foul I fare and painting is my shame' – the poem he wrote about it?"

Maria continued to try and distract Michael from the 'Last Judgement'.

"If you look up, I love the painting of God creating Eve, although it's never remembered. Or the planets, God creates Adam is always the one they show over and over again. Even David slaying Goliath in the corner is never discussed."

Michael turned to Maria. Slaying was what he heard in his head.

"Where?"

"Up there in the top right corner, between Joel and Zacheriah."

Michael's eyes wandered to the next painting of Moses and then across the middle. All of the paintings were adorned with god-like men, naked almost welcoming him into the fold.

"I need a drink."

"I think that is a good idea." Maria grabbed another couple of glasses off the table and Michael drank his second straight down.

They spent the next fifteen minutes in the chapel. Maria had tried to deflect his gaze but with little joy. They were then all ushered off to a small room at the side of the chapel where preparations had been made for dinner.

It was a quiet affair with several exclusive guests, none that Michael was interested in meeting. At $250,000 a head it was not the scene Michael liked to be in so he began to drink faster and faster. Maria could sense his uncomfortableness, the place had got to him and he was beginning to unravel. Before coffee arrived she had made their excuses and got him outside into the fresh air. They walked back along the museum wall and into St Peter's Square. Harry was about twenty feet behind them now.

"Are you okay now?"

"Yeah, I am fine; I just got a little hot in there."

"I know you don't particularly like that place. I am sorry I made you go. But Mum did insist."

"It's not that I don't like that place, there is something about it, something about the religion and the paintings and the history. It gets me wound up; it's like as soon as my blood boils so do I."

Maria didn't know what to say to him, he was being reflective and open at the same time and this was rare for Michael.

"Is there something wrong with me?" Maria certainly didn't know how to answer that question.

"You see when I am in there, in the museum or the chapel, the paintings, the tapestries, the sculptures, they picture death, destruction, the half-naked men everywhere, it brings a longing in me or a desire, but if I was to walk through to St Peter's Basilica, the Chair of Saint Peter, the Cherub Holy Water Font, St Andrew, Helena, St Peter; they all scream religion to me and a calmness about who and what we are. The monument of innocence that is in there, I look at that every time I go in and is it an accident that the monument is of children and women? Sure the pope is reigning over them but does it mean man is not innocent and was never meant to be?"

Maria was still quiet. She checked to see if Harry was still behind them as this was something that Michael had never done. He had never talked to her about questioning himself and what he was.

"The statue of truth is another one; think it's on the right as you go in. It's truth standing on the world holding the gates to eternity, but the only reason eternity is standing is that death is holding it all together, or so I would presume."

They walked around the square in silence for the next ten minutes, Maria too scared to say anything and Michael contemplating God and who he was.

"How about a coffee, it will make us feel better. That cafe you like is just over there by the taxi rank and Harry can go and fetch the car for when we are finished."

Michael smiled at Maria, his thoughts and life were only better when she was close to him. "Sounds good to me."

Alex woke up on the sofa; it had been a month since she had done that. A month that had changed her life. She packed away the computer and tucked the hard drive back into her gun case and then into the laptop bag in order for it to be safe. 'She would have a quick shower, get dressed and then go over to her parents' house. She was keen to get there long before Chris did so she could set the scene. As she pulled up outside the house she checked her phone; she expected to see a dozen messages from Chris on there asking how she was, and conversely she had one message, from a withheld number. It had to be Michael. It simply read: 'Goodnight'. Michael had sat up drinking long after Maria had gone to bed and Alex was his last thought before going to sleep. He wanted her to know that.

Michael was going to have to wait. This was another afternoon when Alex didn't want to raise suspicion about herself or anything that she had done.

Alex walked up the path way and into the house. Her dad was in the kitchen preparing vegetables.

"Not too many, Dad." As he turned Alex gave him a big hug, holding on just a bit too long to be able to show him that she had really missed him.

"Don't know what you mean, Alex?"

"You do, Dad, you cook as if you are cooking for your whole station. Jason and I used to be eating leftovers on a Wednesday after you had cooked."

"There are more of us now you know, Jason and Sandra and little Ethan. And now I hear even you are bringing a date to Sunday dinner."

"Not a date, Dad, just a friend who I think needs feeding up." Alex kissed him on the cheek. "Where's Mum?"

"In the yard hanging out the washing, you know she can't keep still when I am in her kitchen."

Alex walked out into the yard to see her mum. She walked over and hugged her from behind as she was still hanging out her dad's shirts.

"How are you, dear?"

"I am good, been a very long few weeks but I am glad things will start to return to normal now."

"Me too, so sad about Sophie." Alex's mum never pushed any of her family to answer questions about cases or police work. But Sophie had meant more than that to Alex so she deserved a mention. With a whole family of police officers she figured they would talk when they needed to and she was always here for that. They in turn protected her from the real world as much as possible.

"So Chris?"

"I know, Mum. I also know what you will be thinking but it's early days and I think after the week we have all had it would be good to share some time with one of Dad's roast dinners."

"You know he has done five lots of vegetables, I have told him to stop. We will be eating it for months; we don't even have you and your brother here all the time to get through them any more."

"Alex." Jason stood on the porch with a beer in his hand; Alex could see Sandra and Ethan in the kitchen with her dad.

Alex ran towards him and hugged him closer than most, Jason was a big guy and he could take a proper squeezing. It had been far too long since they had been together.

"What was that for?"

"Nothing, dufus, I am just giving hugs out today."

"Can I get one of those then?" Sandra was now out on the porch whilst Ethan had been roped into peeling carrots.

Sandra and Jason had been high school sweethearts, there wasn't a more open and loving couple. Jason was clearly punching above his weight band with Sandra and Alex never missed an opportunity to tell him. Jason doted on her; Sandra and Ethan were his world. It had been a reflection of their childhood. Their parents knew just the right balance of freedom and discipline and always did everything with love. It made Jason want to be like his dad. He worked with him and was tipped to be the next captain after his dad retired.

"Of course." Alex hugged Sandra.

"I hear we have another guest coming," she whispered in her ear.

"It's not like it's the first time I have brought someone over is it?" Alex almost shouted it loud enough for everyone to hear.

"This is true, Hun, my little sister's brought lots of guys by. There was Billy Minchin, came over for dinner and then they played on the swings all afternoon aged ten, Robert Robertson, who calls their son Robert Robertson why I will never know? But he was here for two Sundays in a row aged fourteen. Shall I go on?"

Alex thumped him in the arm and disappeared into the kitchen to hug Ethan. Alex's mum nodded at them to follow, she was worried about Alex although she would never say it, and she knew that a family dinner would be exactly what they needed. They sat in the kitchen taking turns to talk stories of how messed up they all were whilst Dad made dinner until Chris came. Alex introduced him to Sandra, Ethan and her mother and they sat at the table to eat.

"So, Chris, how is work?"

"You know the rule, Fred, no talking police work at the dinner table."

"It's not police work it's criminology, or medical examiner, it's different."

"Well there is not much to talk about to be fair. I am sure Alex has filled you all in on our trip to Germany, which is about the highlight of the year for me." Alex had mentioned it but only in passing, she didn't want to go into the detail or to get her family involved in what was going on.

"She did mention it briefly, so nothing else?"

"No, in fact with your daughter she isn't really giving me enough time. She solved the Gordon case this week within hours, doesn't really need the ME to get involved."

"Alex, Gordon case? You said it was a quiet week?" Jason and Alex always shared cases, she was his confidant. Even above Paul, she would always call Jason first so as not to seem stupid in front of Paul.

"I was just lucky that is all, it was Thursday and I went to question."

"Re question," Chris pointed out.

"Re question a person in the building and he just started to fidget and get nervous. I kept probing him and before I knew it he was making for the door."

"Policewoman's instinct, her partner James had been to see the same guy the day before and come back with nothing."

"Well done, honey, now that is enough police talk at the table, you lot."

Alex's mum started passing the potatoes around. "Eat more else I am going to be eating this for a week." They all laughed.

"So, Alex, what have you been up to? Did you see the game yesterday?" Alex looked directly at Jason and then again at Chris.

"It was good, wasn't it, Dad. I came over yesterday and we watched it out on the porch." Alex had lied to Chris and said she was visiting her family yesterday. She needed an excuse. Chris was looking at her; she could feel it, although she didn't want to make eye contact.

"I was coming over too, but I got side tracked. I ended up looking at old photos all day of me, Paul, Sophie. Guess I was lost to my memories."

Chris grabbed her hand under the table; that had worked. The rest of the dinner was of more pleasant conversation. The story about Robert Robertson and Billy Minchin made its second airing just to embarrass Alex and over dessert her mother even brought out the family album.

After saying their goodbyes Chris followed Alex back to her apartment. "If you had wanted I would have come over yesterday."

"I know, I slept in till about noon, finished tidying and putting some washing on and then sat reminiscing."

"I can tell." Chris pointed to the three empty bottles of wine on the side.

"I tipped half of the third one away." Alex could hear the words coming out of her mouth as she said them. She had been defending her drinking to Chris, she couldn't quite understand if it was a defence mechanism or she actually didn't want him to think less of her.

"And what's the box for?" Chris headed over to the side. Alex had to get there before him so she almost leapt across him to get to it.

"It's just some private memories."

"Oh okay." Chris stood back.

"Are you okay, Alex? Something seems to be a little off lately. Don't get me wrong, I am loving the new Alex, in fact I think I may be loving her a little too much. I just want to know that you are okay?"

"Yeah, I am okay, been a long few weeks."

"I know, I know."

Chris walked over and put his arms around Alex. "I know we didn't get the answers we wanted out of Germany, or the Quaid case, but we need to let them go now and move on." Alex couldn't move on. She had all the answers, what she didn't have was a plan about what to do with them without building suspicion around herself. Jack's letter and the hard drive she got from Dee were enough to change the world.

"Things will go back to the way they were soon, I hope."

"I hope not."

Chris leant down and kissed Alex. Alex knew it was time for a distraction. Chris was getting worried and worry can turn into questions.

Chapter 7

It was Chris's turn to leave Alex in bed sleeping. Her alarm was set for eight and Chris had been gone for an hour before she woke up. He had a morning's work in the IT department and then he was on a medical refresher course.

Alex had masked over her black eye yesterday with makeup which was now all over the pillow. After last night's activities she ensured she was face down asleep when Chris left.

A shower and a touch up on the makeup before heading into the station. Her aim was to get in front of the captain before anyone else did. This didn't work, as she walked into her office the captain, Chris and James were all waiting for her.

"My office, now."

She knew this wasn't going to go down well, not only with the captain but with Chris also.

"Close the door." James was the last one in and closed the door behind him.

The captain sat behind the desk, Alex was expecting to hear the sound of his booming voice any minute but she didn't.

"Are you okay?"

"Yes, I am fine."

"What happened?" Alex had to presume Chris already knew as the look on his face was one of complete disappointment.

"I took a drive, that's all."

"Alex, three men are in the morgue by your hand, a woman has been saved and we have at least five more bodies in the bar?"

"Five?"

"Five, there was a guy in the cellar, and four what I presume used to be bikers in the dumpster out back."

Deacon James had been a busy guy, he hadn't lied to Alex about how many girls he had killed, it was twenty-six, what he didn't say was that in the last twenty years he had killed three times as many men, just for fun.

"I didn't know about them."

"Alex, I spoke to the police chief this morning. They are saying he may be the biggest single serial killer since Adolf Hitler, they have a string of men and women up and down the country with his DNA all over them."

"Twenty-six women."

"What?" James always wanted to get one reaction into every meeting he had with the captain. Just so that he noticed he was still there as he tended to blend into the background.

"Twenty-six women, he conf... bragged about it to me. Just as he was going to do the same to me, but I managed to get free and grab my weapon."

"Alex, you didn't just get free you put them all in the morgue."

"Captain, it was me or them, it truly was."

Alex was getting emotional now. She could feel that there was a tension in the air from everyone; she had been caught lying by Chris, she didn't really consider it lying, more not telling the truth. She didn't call the captain as soon as it happened or her partner which she should have done.

"I have no doubt of that, Alex, but that is five murderers caught in two days. You are cleaning up the streets single handedly, why didn't you call?"

"Yes, why didn't you call?" Chris didn't mean the captain, he meant him, why didn't you call him. After everything they had been through.

"I was going to, I got home early hours of Saturday morning and slept, and when I woke I was still playing it all over in my head, wondering how I escaped and how I got the better of them. I am not proud of it, but I locked my front door and tried to drink away the memory. If I hadn't have seen them slip something into my drink I would have been number twenty-eight."

Alex knew the right words to push people's buttons. Chris was now thinking twice about his, 'why didn't you call' comment. They all knew how hard these circumstances were, especially given there were sixty-eight years' worth of police work in that office.

"Twenty-eight?"

"Yes, James, twenty-eight, I didn't know they had someone already upstairs tied up on a mattress on the floor.. It wasn't until the place was completely silent I could hear some banging."

"Leave us." The captain nodded at Chris and James. Chris didn't want to leave; he wanted answers to his own questions. Like how did we spend the last twenty-four hours together and you didn't mention that you were set upon by a gang of murderers and nearly died? Reluctantly they both left the office.

"What do you want me to do, Alex? I tried ringing you this morning and couldn't get you, so I rang your father? He knew nothing about it, neither him nor your brother? He told me neither of you mentioned it, neither of you as Chris was at your parents for dinner yesterday? Don't get me wrong, Alex, I like Chris, but you never have. What is going on with you?"

Alex was stumped for an answer. The captain was right. She and Chris weren't close. They had started to become closer but out of a need for companionship, nothing else. She hadn't told her parents or her brother; this wasn't going to go down well with them. They had a rule in the house that they shared all this between the three of them. Any major events in their careers they had to discuss as a family and she had kept this from them.

"I don't think you are ready to return to work, Alex, something is clearly happening with you. I don't know what it is but you need to sort it out."

"Not ready? How can I not be ready, I have caught five murderers in a few weeks."

"Yes and four are dead in a bar up state and one survived, but honestly, I think that if he had run, he would not have. Alex you have lost your partner and his wife in the last six months, started a relationship with someone I was convinced was your arch enemy, become obsessed with a suicide case to the extent that you chartered a flight halfway around the world. Lied to your colleagues and your family and me? You are an amazing detective, Alex, you really are, but at the moment I think your head is in the wrong place."

"I didn't lie."

"No, you just didn't tell the truth. Your dad said he didn't have a clue, Alex, and the man is Captain. He is trained to pick up on these things."

Alex was looking directly at the ground as she didn't know where else to look. She couldn't stop doing what she was doing, the work was so important. It was starting to take over her life. It was her life.

"I have no choice, Alex, I am going to put you on a two week leave and when you return you will have to go through a week's worth of counselling with Dr Lee and then we will decide what you will do."

"But the case, the Deacon James murders, they will need me." Alex was fighting to stay at work. At least here she had the resources to carry on with the list. There would be little she could do from home.

"Why will they? It's not like you knew them, or that any one of them is left standing, you killed them all."

Alex started to feel that fighting was going to be useless. The captain had made up his mind and it's what she would have done in his position. She stood up and turned towards the door.

"Alex, if you need anything you just call me. Or at least talk to someone about this."

"Yes, Captain."

Alex closed the door behind her, she didn't want to face any more questions, and she could see James and Chris in the office waiting for her return. It was easier to slip out of the door; she was still carrying her laptop bag from the ambush when she walked in.

Alex left the station and went to the coffee shop across the road. She ordered a coffee and Danish and sat in the window. This had been the same coffee shop she sat in to read Dee's letter to Jack back when this case was still just a suicide, she found herself thinking how the world had changed in the last month. She had committed murder, on more than one occasion and today she had been suspended pending approval from the doctor to be able to return to work. Alex needed a plan. She needed to get this all back on track and start to work through Jack's stolen files.

Pulling her phone from her jacket pocket, there had been a missed call from the captain and a dozen missed calls from her family and

Chris, and they had all tried to contact her before and after the meeting with the captain.

Also, there was another text message, from the withheld number. It just read: 'Can't wait to see you x'. That made up Alex's mind, whilst she couldn't deal with everything that was going on with work, Chris and her family right now, there was one thing she could deal with.

Michael woke early Sunday morning. He checked up on Maria, she was sleeping soundly in her own room. As they were only a ten to fifteen minute walk to Vatican Square he decided to take a walk there. Last night was still fresh in his mind and he was trying to make sense of who he was and where his place in the world was. Without saying a word he left the apartment and set off, closely followed by Harry. Harry was there for his protection and as protection from himself. Maria was going to be fine on her own. She didn't need Harry and his orders were clear when it came to Michael. Michael paid his money and went directly into the Basilica. He sat at the back of the church on the last row of fold out chairs. Harry remained at the door. For an hour Michael just looked at the floor, deep in thought about his next move. He had the odd glance at the statues and people surrounding him. But generally he was just checking to see if Harry was still behind him. He was.

After an hour Michael walked the Basilica, all the sculptures and paintings he had discussed with Maria last night, it was as if he was looking at them for one more time, studying every inch of them. The Pieta, a statue of Mary and Christ, kept resonating in his mind. He could see himself in the statue in Maria's arms. She had been the glue that had kept him together for so long and he knew in the end this is what was going to happen. He would be dying and she would be comforting him. Michael lost half a day to daydreams and fantasies in the Basilica before returning to Maria.

"Where have you been?"

"Me and Harry took a walk together in the sunshine."

"Have you had breakfast? Do you want to go and get some lunch?"

"I am fine, let's go out and have lunch; there is that little Italian restaurant opposite the Forum on the left hand side of the road."

"I think they just call them restaurants here," Maria said with a smile.

"Yes, they do. Let's do that and then have a walk around the Forum."

"Then the Coliseum?"

"No, still not yet. I am saving that."

Alex was back at her apartment; she picked up the flight tickets and the hotel details and packed a bag. In the bag she packed Michael and Maria's file, her laptop and the hard drive, a couple of changes of clothes and some toiletries. She kept thinking of Jack and his go bag in the airport locker. She was about to go to a second country in a month. For someone who had been out of the country only once before this, this was an extreme change for her. Her only previous trip had been a long weekend in England with Paul and Sophie, meeting Paul's parents for the first time. It had been his uncle's fiftieth birthday party and they all attended.

The ride to the airport was a short one and within two hours she was sitting in first class being offered champagne for the take off.

"Michael, don't you just love people watching." Maria and Michael sat outside the restaurant. They could see the bustle of people on the opposite side of the road, heading into the Forum or heading towards the Coliseum. There were buskers and artists dotting in and out of them and looky looky men all selling selfie sticks at five euros a pop.

"More than life itself." This was true for both of them. As kids they would love to sit and make up the stories of the people walking past. That couple are having a divorce as she was walking ten paces behind him. The letchy man over there is a serial rapist, that's why he can't take his eyes off every woman passing.

They both had a knack for this type of thing. They were very good at reading other people. Michael could tell a liar from a thousand paces. And when it came to each other they could tell exactly how the other was feeling. It was why Maria was worried about Michael. Something was changing in him, and she wasn't sure it was for the better. His questions last night and his behaviour over the last couple of days had been more erratic and somehow more reflective.

"How was the pasta? You have hardly touched it?"

"It was fine, Maria; I am just not that hungry."

"Are you ready for dessert or a walk?"

"You have dessert and I will go and get the tickets."

"Okay, get the ones that you can access the coliseum and the forum and we can use the other one tomorrow?"

"Okay, Harry can wait with you."

Harry ignored Michael. He had his orders. He followed twenty paces behind him as Michael walked to the Coliseum and bought some tickets. The queue took longer than expected and by the time he had got back dessert was done and Maria had settled the bill.

"Ready?"

"Ready."

They spent the afternoon walking and talking through the Forum. Maria's imagination was great, she could really bring the market to life again with her stories and the Roman lifestyle fascinated Michael. The rawness of the market place, Caesar's Temple, the Temple of Saturn, the allure of the Coliseum; all those things made Michael wish this had been the time when he was born.

Maria quoted history as if she was a tour guide, and Michael was most at ease when he could hear her voice, especially when she was excited and passionate about something. He metamorphosed himself into her, her love for life, her smile, everything about Maria screamed love, life, happiness. Michael knew he wasn't good for her though. Michael wasn't good or happy; everything about him screamed death and destruction. He needed to do something about that for the both of them. His head for the first time had started to think that they were better off apart. He didn't want Maria to continue in his world as it was getting a darker place and she was better than that. She deserved better than that.

Michael suggested a late supper and an early night, Maria was delighted with this. She knew that if he was home with her then there would be no altercations elsewhere. Sunday was indeed the day of rest and after supper he and Maria cuddled up and watched a movie together on Michael's laptop. The extremes from one day to another were starting to worry Maria but for now she was thankful of the change. Thankful that Michael was home and safe with her.

Chapter 8

Leonardo da Vinci airport was sixteen miles south of Rome. Because of the time difference in flights Alex arrived at three thirty in the afternoon, four and a half hours before she was due to meet Michael. It was a long flight and she had little sleep but she kept awake with coffee and energy drinks. She knew she was going to need her wits about her tonight.

On arrival into Rome she checked into the hotel. It was a short ten minute walk to the Coliseum from where she was, her hotel was almost underneath the church of San Pietro in Vincoli. Alex refused the bell boy and carried her own bags to the room. When she unlocked the room she was hesitant, thinking that Michael would already be inside. He wasn't, although there was a bottle of champagne on the side and a note re-enforcing the time for her to be at the Coliseum and welcoming her to Rome. She thought Michael must have been convinced she would come, even though she hadn't been.

Michael hadn't been convinced either but he put an alert at the airport that if she was picked up to leave the note and the champagne. Michael was still back in the apartment in bed sleeping on and off whilst watching TV in his room. Maria had been the early bird this morning and spent the morning shopping.

Alex changed and decided to take a walk to clear her head. She didn't need a drink of the champagne that Michael had left her, coffee was what she needed. She grabbed a local map from reception and the receptionist had pointed out how close she was to the statue of Moses and it seemed as good a place to start as any. Alex walked up the hundred plus steps to the square outside the church. There was a waffle and coffee vendor outside and the first thing she did was sit on the steps and drink a coffee. It was hot and sunny; she felt there was something calming about the sunshine. Alex felt more focused.

Outside, the building could almost be mistaken for a shopping mall with big arches on the entrance. Inside was a different matter. Alex believed it to be the most beautiful church she had ever seen. Given that most churches she had been in were two hundred years old at most and for funerals and weddings, she didn't really have a lot to go on. The sheer size of the inside and the altar and roof had her in amazement. The Moses statue was to the front right of the church, a masterpiece hidden away from all the others in Rome. If you didn't know to go looking for it, it wasn't something you would wander past. Inside were the chains of St Peter, which was what the church was named after and tapestries on the walls. Alex felt a sense of honesty and loyalty from the church. The silence was unnerving. Anyone giving this much dedication to make these paintings, sculptures and tapestries to religion must have truly believed. Before leaving she went to the fountain and made the sign of the cross in holy water, something she had never done before but she felt as if it was needed.

It was a short walk up the road to the Basilica Papale di Santa Maria Maggiore. Alex still wanted to see more and to keep her mind off the eight p.m. deadline that was looming towards her.

Alex had been wrong. This was the most beautiful church she had ever been in; she couldn't help thinking, if these were just local ones to her hotel, what does the Vatican look like? She had read all about it on the plane and St Peter's Basilica. They hadn't even mentioned these places in the magazine.

The walls were covered with paintings and mosaics; Moses was prominent here also, getting the Jews out of Egypt. The crypt of the nativity, the reliquary of the holy crib, all of it filled Alex with a sense of humbleness. There was a service going on in Italian, Alex didn't understand it but sat and listened with the hundred or so people who were in there also.

Alex donated to each box as she walked around, again it felt like an obligation, and again before she left she made the sign of the cross with the holy water at the entrance. It was time.

Michael had cooked an early dinner for Maria. She had returned from shopping and Michael had set the table on the balcony.

"Good day shopping?"

"Yes, thank you, Michael, you didn't have to do all this? But I bought you some shirts and a tie." Maria pulled out a couple of bags and passed the tie to him.

"It's lovely, Maria, and nonsense – if we can't spoil each other in Rome where and when can we? Besides, that is what big brothers are for."

"Less of the little sister, you, two minutes."

"Two minutes is two minutes. Wine my dear?"

"Don't mind if I do."

Michael pulled out the chair and Maria sat down. He pushed her chair in, draped a napkin across his arm and poured the wine. Maria loved to see Michael happy and he seemed to be elated this evening.

"You look like you have had a good day too."

92

"I have, it's been great. I did some reading, sleeping, watching TV on the laptop, me and Harry went shopping for food and supplies. I have made us a lovely meal."

"Harry, where is Harry?"

"Think he is in his room, even he needs to rest every now and again."

Maria took another sip of her wine. As she did her head became all fuzzy and her vision started to blur. "Michael I don't feel…" Maria dropped the glass and it smashed on the table. Michael grabbed her before she hit the table. Pulling the chair back he placed Maria carefully on the sofa and laid her as if asleep.

"It's going to be fine; you are just going to take a little nap."

Normally the glass shattering would have brought Harry racing through the door. But not now, Harry had let his guard down for a second and took a drink from Michael. He had been watching him cook in the kitchen and was sidetracked for one moment. Michael had been relaxed all morning, chatting, smiling, friendly, it took Harry by surprise.

Deacon James hadn't been the only user of rohipnol, since the quarterback in the bar that got the better of Michael. Michael had a supply just for cases like this. It had taken two pills to take down Harry and he still put up a fight. Carrying him to the room to lay him out had taken Michael a good twenty minutes.

"I love you, Maria, no matter what happens just know that I love you." Michael kissed her on the forehead and Maria could just about hear those words as she gave in to the influence of the drug.

Michael grabbed a backpack that he had already assembled and headed out the door. If Harry had been watching what supplies he had been buying today it would have been a different outcome, but he wasn't. It was time.

Alex headed down the road towards the Coliseum. It was a short walk under a bridge and at the end of the road there were some steps that led her down to the main gates of the Coliseum. Everything looked deserted, apart from the lights were still on in every archway and she could see the odd security person walking around.

Alex went down the steps and stood by the front gates. She hadn't really thought what to expect. Was Michael just going to turn up like they were on a date? Send a limo? She didn't have to wait long. One of the security staff approached her asking if she was Detective Keaton. Michael had arranged for a private tour of the underground in the Coliseum. He had left instructions for her to be escorted to the front and he had scheduled to meet her in there.

This is what he had been doing whilst Maria was finishing dessert yesterday and Harry was set back. The time hadn't been the queuing The reason it had taken so long was that Michael wanted a private viewing of the Coliseum.

Alex entered the front gates and was shown around the Coliseum to the other side and down the stairs. She was underneath the main stage area. The floor over years had disappeared and it was now a maze of walls where the gladiators and animals rose from. You could see straight up to where all the spectators and emperors sat to watch the games.

"It's beautiful, isn't it?" Alex spun around but she could not see anyone. "It's my favourite place in the whole wide world. One thousand nine hundred and thirty plus years and still standing."

"Michael, why am I here?"

"Trajan, who was the thirteenth Emperor of Rome was said to have had games here that lasted a hundred and twenty-three days, with eleven thousand gladiators and ten thousand animals where few survived. Can you imagine that? Eleven thousand people murdered in cold blood. Leopards, tigers, lions, even giraffes and hippos got a shout, at the games."

"So you wanted to give me a history lesson, is that it?"

"No, I am sorry, Detective, I am not the history teacher, my sister on the other hand, she could be. She knows all about this stuff. I just listen to her."

Alex started to walk amongst the walls. She could hear Michael's voice and he was close. She wanted to look at him straight in the eye. She unclipped the gun on her belt but she didn't feel as if he was going to attack. No, he had something else in mind for her.

"Oh, your sister is here too is she? Is she here with us?"

"No, Detective, just you and me, she is home taking a little nap." Something about the way that Michael said that was unnerving to Alex. Was it a nap or 'a nap'?

"It's funny they don't really mention any fights after about 450 AD but I am sure they carried on. They started in 80 AD and if they could kill twenty-one thousand in a hundred and twenty-three days, what do you think, Alex, that makes a possible circa twenty-two million lives lost in this arena – let's call it twenty million for good behaviour."

"Oh, you have brought me to Rome to kill me?" Alex actually didn't believe that was on his agenda for this evening. Michael wanted to play cat and mouse for a while first. He was treating this as some kind of game with her.

"Isn't it kill or be killed in this world, Detective?"

"In your world, Michael, only in your world."

95

Alex jumped as she thought she saw Michael turning a corner. It had been the shadow of a security guard above her circling the Coliseum.

"No, Detective, I am not here to kill you, not today. Besides I paid for the tour on my credit card, even I am not as sloppy as that."

"I wouldn't be your first though, would I, Michael?" There was a pause after that question. Michael wasn't ready to answer.

"Do you know it's now one of the new seven wonders of the world. New and nearly two thousand years old? Like the Taj Mahal and the Great Wall of China."

Alex approached every corner as if it was going to bring her face to face with Michael. "You didn't answer my question, Michael?"

"Sorry, didn't I? How is your new partner, James is it? Not your new sexual partner Chris. Your actual partner, in crime fighting?"

Alex stopped in her tracks, how did he know about Chris? Nobody at work knew other than the captain and that was only this morning.

"Answer the question, Michael; I would not be your first?"

"Answer the question, Detective. Did it take two men to do the job Paul was doing for you behind his wife's back?"

Alex's heartbeat was racing, how dare he talk about Paul, that's not for him to know. Paul wasn't doing anything behind Sophie's back, she hadn't slept with Paul.

"I guess his brother wasn't up to much either the other night as he flew straight back home after your brief encounter in the hotel."

"Michael, come out where I can see you." Alex was shouting now as he was getting confident with his words. "How did you know about that, are you having me followed?"

"Know your enemy, Detective, that is all. I know you have a problem with me, I know you want revenge for that attack the other night and I know you think I have done worse."

"I know, Michael. What I know is everything."

"You think you do, did you know about, and yes before you ask I am changing the subject, did you know that 1200 AD this was used as a castle and they had great banqueting halls just here? Not as big as your dinner yesterday by the way with your mum and dad, and I want to say Jason, Sandra, Ethan and Paul too, sorry Chris."

Michael had gone too far, Alex's gun was now in front of her.

"Detective, just as I wouldn't get away with it, no point pulling your gun. What would they say back home, you hunted me down from America to here and shot an unarmed man in cold blood. Especially after they realise that I invited you as a thank you for saving my life."

"Don't talk about my family, Michael, this is between you and me, you forget I know what you are."

"And what am I, Detective?"

Alex stopped in her tracks. On the floor in front of her was a speaker, she hadn't noticed it but she had already walked past a couple of them. She hadn't been looking at the ground, she had been concentrating on what might come around the corner. Michael wasn't down there with her, he was on the next level or the one above that. The Coliseum could hold eighty-seven thousand people, he could be anywhere that had a bird's eye view of her walking around.

"You are a killer, Michael, it's in your genes."

Michael laughed at her. "That's what you think do you?"

"That's what I know, Michael, you just don't do you? You don't know what you are? You don't know what they did to you?"

"What who did to me?" Michael's voice became louder.

Alex thought back to the promise that she had made to Christopher and Carly about not revealing to Michael and Maria who they were. But that was before he started playing this little game. That was before he started following her and threatening the people that she loved.

"Now you want to talk, Michael, come here. You want to know what they did to you at birth, why Maria is so sweet, so loving, so gentle and you, you are dark and a monster capable of hurting people, killing people? You want to know these things then come and face me, rather than hiding behind your speakers and your phone."

Alex had pushed the one button that Michael had, the one question that he had been asking himself for years, why wasn't he more like Maria. Michael's rage had started to build up but he knew she was armed and he wasn't. He hadn't set out to kill her today, no matter how appealing it was now. He just wanted to play with her and frighten her a little to see if she would back off but it wasn't going to plan.

"Michael, cat got your tongue?"

"You are making stuff up, Detective, to see if you can rattle me, like I rattled you, fair play."

"It's not made up, Michael, I have yours and Maria's files right here, here it tells you everything, everything you really are."

"I am not playing your little game, Detective."

"Oh you will, Michael, you know you are different, you know there is something wrong with you, you recognise that yourself. When you were on the floor of the nightclub crying like a little girl, you confessed you knew what you were about to do, if it wasn't for your sister and father I would have had you locked up already."

"Then why didn't you follow it through, Detective, it is all just words. You have nothing so I am not playing this game."

"I didn't because I knew there was more to this; I wanted your father's help to find out what they were doing. Not just to you, what they had done to all of you. I wanted to prove once and for all what you were."

Michael was now enraged. He knew that his father had let her have the plane, he never asked but he presumed it was some kind of bribe to let him get away with the stabbing in the nightclub. He was used to his father making things go away.

"It's right here, Michael, all you have to do is come and get it."

Michael was on the first level in the far corner of the Coliseum. He could see Alex walking around with a file, she wasn't kidding. She had something. And he wanted it. Problem was, there was a gun in one hand and a file in the other.

"You are a murderer, Michael, you were born to be a murderer and you will die a murderer."

"Michael? Are you still there? Want to know where you were born, want to know how you were born, you were a little fish in a big dish, Michael, just as you are today."

"We are done for today, Detective." Michael turned off the speakers, Alex was carrying one in her hand and she could see the red light go out.

Alex climbed onto the closest wall to scour around above her but the light had started to fade and she couldn't see anything.

"Michael, don't you want this? Don't you want to know who you are?"

Alex was getting the silent treatment. She could just about make out two security guards on the top level who were walking the Coliseum. She was alone on the bottom level. Michael had gone.

Alex put the file back into her back pack. She knew she was going to end up using it; it was her only leverage on Michael which would knock him off track, which it certainly did. Alex hadn't kept her promise to Christopher, but she didn't feel that was going to be a problem, he was someone that she would not be seeing again as this was going to end one way or another. Either she would end up another of Michael's victims or he would end up one of hers.

Alex left the Coliseum through the main gates and headed over to the steps up to the main road leading to her hotel. As she reached the second landing area of the steps a figure stood out from the shadow. She didn't have the time to reach for her gun before she was hit across the head and knocked to the ground. She blacked out before hitting the floor.

Chapter 9

Alex was revived on the steps by a security guard who had been locking up after their visit. She had been lying there for about thirty minutes. Michael had watched her leave the Coliseum and knowing the location of the hotel he hid in the shadows in order to surprise her. After he knocked her out he stood above her for a moment realising that he could just as easily kill her here and now. But it was too risky, even for him. Maria and Harry weren't there to help cover his tracks. He would have still been the last person with her so the last person of interest. His credit card had him linked to her and the security guard would testify that she was the person he had been waiting for. Michael made it away with the backpack which only had the files inside.

Alex told the security guard that she must have tripped up a step. She knew it was Michael and he now had the file. There was little she was going to be able to do about that. She just needed to get back to the hotel. She walked along the road, headed into the hotel and stood in the reception area.

There was a bar to the right hand side of the reception, she walked across and ordered a large brandy. Not her normal drink but she needed something stronger to help her deal with the events of the day. She then went back to her room and lay on the bed. Within minutes her eyes were closed and she was asleep, part exhaustion part concussion.

Michael ran from the steps and headed up towards the Pantheon. It was five to ten minutes running, the night was still early and people were still heading out for dinner.

The small Irish bar, the Scholars Lounge, was on the way. Michael ran in there and ordered a drink. To the right of the entrance there were two little booths with their own TVs in for privacy. The band was still setting up so he got his drink and sat in the nearest booth to the door with the backpack.

Opening it he pulled out two files; one for him and one for Maria. He laid them next to each other. Alex was telling the truth. She had something on Michael and Maria.

He opened his own file and started to read through it, there were some pieces around his mother and his father and the date they were born. In bold letters The Brown Institute, Paris, stood out. Christopher and Carly hadn't lied about being born in Paris but they did lie about where. They hadn't really been prepared for the question one night over dinner when the twins were about twelve, and not knowing the names of any other hospitals they made up a story about being late back from the theatre and giving birth to them in a hotel room with an ambulance arriving in time to help. They had even taken Michael and Maria back to the hotel to show them the room. His parents created a whole ruse, their names Michael and Maria were from the play they had been watching. The story had been so believable but they had been lying to him all this time.

Michael read through all the records, he remembered the checkups, but he had been lied to about why they were needed. For school, for college, just because we love you, Michael – all lies. But the files didn't say anything about him being born a murderer. Alex had said he was born to be a murderer, the files didn't say he was a murderer and certainly didn't say Maria was.

Alex didn't move quickly enough, she could hear the lock on the door but she was still half asleep before Michael was in the room. He had booked the room, why didn't she think that it was only common sense that he would have asked for another key.

Before she knew it he was on top of her, pinning her to the bed. "How? How do you know what I am?" Michael was shouting, his temper was getting the better of him. "How do you know I am different? There is nothing in those files. I have read them cover to cover, there is no difference between me and Maria."

Alex was struggling to get up and away from him. He had his knees on her chest and he was holding her arms down on the bed.

"How, Alex?" Michael was at the top of his voice now which had started a chain of calls to the front desk.

"The code, Michael, look at the code on the front. P&M, you are a psychopathic murderer, Maria compassionate and loyal, C&L. It's in the code they used."

Michael got off Alex and grabbed the backpack. It was there in black and white as she had mentioned it. He just hadn't noticed it before.

"How do I know you didn't just write that on there? How do I know?"

Michael had a point. Alex knew that would be the question everyone would have asked of the files, it didn't really prove anything. Not without the hard drive and more details on each person.

"Because, because I have more, Michael. You are not the only one, there are thousands of these." Alex was standing now, with one foot back to ensure that if he rushed her she was ready for him this time.

"Excuse me." The night porter had entered the room as Michael was standing by the desk. Michael could see a crowd of people forming in the hallway also. He took the bag, barged by the porter and ran. Alex jumped up to follow but by the time she had got to the door he had gone.

Alex was looking at the crowd that had gathered. She couldn't chase him, but she was now worried about what she had done. The thoughts she had been having around, if you tell someone they are a killer they live up to expectation, were about to be proved or disproved.

The night porter was more concerned over Alex. She made up a story about him being an ex boyfriend and was there any way that she could change rooms as she was worried about him returning. The staff were all apologetic, and upgraded her room; they had given him a key without thinking.

Michael was back running again, but this time towards home. It was twenty-five minutes away and all he could think about was what Alex had said, he was starting to unravel. All those feelings he had been having all his life were real. He was repressing what he was meant to do, what he was meant to be. All the paintings and tapestries he had been viewing had been telling him to do what he was born to do. There wasn't a doubt in Michael's mind that everything Alex had told him was true. It made sense.

When he opened the door Maria and Harry were both in the living room.

Maria dived in front of Harry to get to Michael. "Don't hurt him, Harry, don't hurt him. Michael, what have you done? Where have you been?"

Maria had hold of Michael with both arms wrapped tightly around him. Harry was three steps away, standing still and saying nothing.

"We had to ring Dad, tell me you have not done anything, tell me Michael, tell me." Maria was bordering on screaming these words at her brother.

"I haven't done anything but they have. Dad, Mum, they have lied to us, Maria, lied to us about all of it."

"All of what?" Michael was mad, she could see it in him. The rage that she feared had returned.

"That detective, Alex, Dad helped her, Dad helped her find out who we are?"

"Michael, you aren't making sense?"

"The Brown Institute, Maria, that's where we were born, not a hotel, not some nice story about theatre. We were some kind of experiment and they knew about it, we were made separately and they changed us, Maria, they changed me."

Harry took three steps back and grabbed his phone from his pocket. He disappeared into the hallway. Harry had been fully briefed on the Brown Institute and he knew this was a game changer. He needed to ring Christopher.

"They changed you how, Michael?"

"I don't know, but Alex told me?"

"Wait, Alex Keaton the detective? Are you saying she is here?"

Michael slowed his breathing down a little. He hadn't told her that he had sent her a ticket. That he had arranged the whole meeting in the Coliseum.

"She said that they made me into a psychopathic murderer and that they gave you the alternative, they made you compassionate and loyal. Don't you see that makes sense, for the first time it makes sense why we are so different."

Maria was trying to deal with a lot of information at one point. Alex was here in Rome, their parents had lied to them and there was a reason why Michael was how he was, that was the main thought going through her head. Michael is what he is because of something else. That was something she had dreamed of. She was almost happy at the thought it wasn't his fault.

"Calm down, Michael, we need to talk to Dad. He will explain everything."

"I have," Harry walked into the room. "He has said that you are to remain here and he will personally be here tomorrow evening to discuss it with you."

"See, Maria, it is true else why would he make the journey all this way? I am the last person he would do that for at the moment. I want to talk to him now." Michael grabbed his phone out of his jacket and started to dial the number.

Harry walked across and took it off him with ease. "No."

"I can talk to my father, Harry."

"He said no phone calls. He will be here tomorrow, that is enough."

"That's because he knows it is true, doesn't he, he knows what they have done to me; you know what they have done to me. He is part of this."

"Michael, calm down." Maria could see that look in his eye, she had seen it before.

"You know what they have done to me, Harry. That's why you are always here, that's why Father has me followed everywhere I go. He knew he created a monster and he needed another monster to guard over it."

Harry just turned his back and headed towards the side to put the phone down. Before Harry had made more than three steps Michael had picked a knife off the table that he had prepared for dinner earlier with Maria and jumped on Harry's back plunging the knife into the side of his neck.

"Michael, no, Harry."

Maria was too late, Harry was on the floor for the second time today from Michael's actions and he wasn't recovering from this one. Harry was trying to grab at the knife but Michael still had hold of it in his neck.

Maria ran over to drag Michael off as he let go. Harry fell to the floor blood splattering everywhere in the room.

"Michael, what have you done?"

"What I was meant to do, don't you see, Maria, this is who I am."

Maria wasn't listening she was on the floor with Harry. She pulled the knife out which just made him bleed out all the quicker.

"We have to go, pack some clothes."

"We have to stay, Father is coming and we need to clear this up. He can help us, Michael. He can help you." Maria didn't even think of calling an ambulance. It had become second nature for her to just try and protect Michael. Harry was bleeding to death in her arms and she was already thinking of how her father could take care of the situation.

"Well, I am not staying. He doesn't want to help me, Maria. He just wants rid of me. I have to go."

Michael left the room, Maria stayed with Harry. He was still breathing or convulsing, she couldn't really tell but she didn't want to leave him alone.

Michael ran to his room, packing a bag with clothes and toiletries. He picked up his passport from the night stand and went back into the living room.

Harry's head was now on Maria's lap and she was crying.

"What have you done, Michael? Harry looked after us, he always looked after us. He didn't deserve this. He was nice. He was my friend, he was our family, Michael."

"You need to come with me."

"No, Michael, I need to wait for Father. And so do you, he needs to help sort this out. He will take care of us."

Michael picked the keys off the side for the town car. He knew he needed to get out of there. Father wasn't going to forgive what he had done to Harry. Harry had been Father's most loyal servant. Michael crossed the line and there was no going back.

"So be it, Maria. You are probably better off without me anyway." Michael left through the front door. Maria sat crying with Harry in her arms breathing his last breath.

Alex slept through till one p.m. It was her phone ringing that woke her. The number was withheld. She presumed that Michael had been reflecting on the events of the night and was coming back to continue the conversations.

"Do you know what you have done?"

"I am sorry?" Alex didn't recognise the voice on the end of the phone.

"Do you know what you have done, Detective? Michael has gone and Harry is dead."

"Maria? Who is Harry?"

"Harry, Detective, was our bodyguard. He is dead because of you. He was more than that, he was my friend." Maria hadn't slept since Michael had left the apartment. She had been too scared to ring her father and wanted to vent some anger at someone. After a while she remembered Harry had taken Michael's phone and found the messages he had been sending to Alex.

"I didn't want any of this, Maria, Michael started it."

Maria was still sobbing down the phone. Her world had been falling apart for hours and she was all alone in a blood drenched apartment.

"Where are you? Where are you, Maria, I will come to you?"

"I am at our parents' place near the Vatican, Via dei Banchi Nuovi."

"I will find it, I am twenty-five minutes away."

Maria was still crying. Alex knew none of this was Maria's fault. She had tried to be all things for all people. Although she was also one of Dr Smith's experiments her only issue was that she was too kind.

Alex went to the bathroom and washed her face. She wasn't a detective here so whatever she got involved with she had no support. She needed to remind herself of that. Some of her actions lately weren't showing her as a law enforcer. She changed her top and headed out of the hotel to the Mellor residence.

Within thirty minutes she found the place and knocked on the door. Maria opened it covered in blood. Maria came straight towards her. Alex's reaction had been to hit out or defend herself but within seconds she knew that's not what she was coming for. She grabbed her and collapsed, her knees giving out and hugging her for support.

Alex ushered her back into the house and closed the door. "Come on, sit down and tell me what happened."

Maria tried to compose herself, she couldn't stop shaking and her throat was dry from all the crying. "I don't know, Michael came in raged with anger about a meeting he had had with you and before I knew it he had stabbed Harry in the neck, packed a bag and was gone."

Alex by now was used to the smell of blood and Maria was covered. She knew this was her fault, she had let the devil out of his cage. Her fear about killers achieving their purpose in life had been answered.

"How are you even here, Detective?"

"Michael sent for me, he has been sending me flowers and on Saturday I received a first class plane ticket with hotel accommodation in the post. I know he is your brother but he is unravelling. I thought it was a cry for help, so I came."

Maria knew he was unravelling too. She had walked St Peter's Square with him a few nights ago and she could tell there was a change in him. He was going to a dark place that even she couldn't bring him back from.

"What was Michael talking about? He said you told him he was born a murderer."

"That's not for now, we need to get you and this cleaned up." Alex couldn't get caught up in this in Italy. Michael had a file now so the truth was out there and could be tracked back to her. Sophie could trace it back to her, so could Deacon James. Alex was taking no chances, she needed this covered up and she needed the file back from Michael.

"Go and shower and change clothes. Get those clothes into a plastic bag and bring them back to me." Alex had the tone of someone you didn't answer back so Maria didn't question her. She had been sitting in the living room with Harry for the last twelve hours unable to move. She needed someone to tell her what to do. Maria did as she was told.

Alex sat in the front room looking at Harry. She had never deconstructed a murder scene before, she kept thinking of all the times she had watched Chris work through the evidence. He could trace every element of what went on by the objects in the room, blood splatters on the furniture – it all needed to be cleaned. Alex went to the bedroom and pulled the sheets off one of the beds. She then wrapped Harry in them. There had been a toolbox under the sink in the kitchen that Christopher had liked to dabble with. Inside it Alex found some tape to tape up the sheets so you couldn't tell what was inside. She then rolled the body out onto the balcony. Being in the penthouse apartment she was confident that no one would see it and the fact that at some point Maria's father would come and deal with it.

Back in the living room Alex pulled up the rug where Harry had been lying and then placed that outside also. She mixed hot water and bleach and started to scrub everything she could see. The knife wound in Harry's neck had hit an artery and it had sprayed everywhere. Alex could see blood splattered on the walls and on the furniture. As she continued the front door opened.

"What the hell is going on?" Christopher Mellor had arrived.

Michael had run from the house to the car. He threw his clothes in the back seat and then sat in the driver's seat as if to drive off, but he couldn't move. He was alone, he had killed Harry and his father was never going to forgive that. His sister had stayed behind rather than follow him. For the first time he had no one. He got back out of the car and headed towards the house. Getting to the front door he could hear his sister crying. He leaned against the door. She wasn't going to be able to forgive him either, he had gone too far. Maria's disapproval would be more than he could bear.

Michael walked back down and headed over to St Peter's Square. It was empty and the few lights lighting up the Vatican spoke to him as if to say that you are no longer welcome. We know what you are Michael and this is a House of God. Michael traced the steps he had taken with Maria two nights previously. The feelings he had from the Vatican Museum were coming back to him, he could feel that rage inside him but now it was somehow different, somehow it was supposed to be there. Alex had told him, it's not your fault. Not in so many words but she had pointed out that they had tampered with him. Alex had released him from his curse. Alex had, but Alex had also just taken his family away from him. If she hadn't have told him, he wouldn't have known. Harry wouldn't be dead, Maria wouldn't hate him, his father wouldn't be mad at him. Alex was to blame, why did she have to come here and tell him all this. Michael had gone back to being a petulant child. He was projecting his problems onto Alex. His problems weren't his problems, they were someone else's. Detective Alex Keaton had ruined his life and he needed to hurt her.

Michael walked back to the car and drove to the hotel that he had put Alex in. He covered his head with a hooded coat and walked through reception. Nobody noticed him, by now it was two a.m. and the night porter was asleep in the back of reception. He crept up the stairs and, opening the door to the room very quietly, he entered. It was empty and any evidence of Alex was gone. He had spooked her. Michael lay down on the bed where she had been lying and sniffed the pillow. He could smell Alex; he was going to be like a bloodhound on her case.

Michael slept, not an easy sleep but a restless one. He dreamt of his father, Maria, Alex. At ten he woke to the sound of the maids walking up and down the corridor. He went back to the car and headed towards the airport, the dreams of last night had helped him to formulate a plan. If Alex was going to take away the people he loved from him, he was going to do the same to her.

Chapter 10

"What have you done, Detective?"

Christopher Mellor entered the apartment followed by three guys in black suits. These were Harry's men. They had been working for Harry for over six years and Alex was on the floor covered in Harry's blood and his body lay on the balcony.

"Dad." Maria came running out of her room, showered and dressed but hair still soaking wet. She ran up to him and flung her arms around him. This defused the situation.

"It's Michael, Dad, he has gone."

Christopher scanned the room. Michael's gone and the detective is on her hands and knees cleaning blood off the floor.

"What?"

"He has gone, he left last night."

"Then whose blood is that?"

Maria turned to look at Alex as if for approval to say whose it was, also noticing that the body was no longer there.

"It was your bodyguard Harry. Michael murdered him last night before leaving. Maria called me this morning and I came over to help." Christopher's rage disappeared from his face and it was replaced with shock for a second, before the anger showed again. All the men wearing suits tensed, somehow it made Alex lean back as if she was about to get the blame.

Still holding onto Maria, Christopher looked down at her. "What happened?"

"I don't know, Michael came home in a rage about meeting with Alex and then the next thing I knew Harry was on the floor with a knife in his neck."

"Detective, stop doing that and explain to me what you think happened."

Alex stood up and explained the events of the last couple of days, from the flowers to the phone calls and the box arriving at the apartment. She stuck with the story that she took it as a cry for help and she was going to ensure that she gave him some. She told Christopher about the meeting in the Coliseum and she explained about the speakers and the fact that they had started to discuss her family.

"I am sorry, Mr Mellor, I know I promised you I wouldn't tell him about the clinic but he started to threaten my family and I wasn't prepared for that." Christopher didn't say anything.

"I don't get it, Detective? We discussed the clinic on your return from Germany, you said you found nothing?"

"And that was true. All along all the evidence that I needed was back in the USA. I had been investigating the suicide of a guy called Jack Quaid. He led me to the files that were in the airport, which led me to you. He had been to Germany and Paris and managed to download a hard drive with all the names and conditions of the patients on. There is a code to what they have been doing. And Jack broke the code before he shot himself."

"Which is what, Detective? What had this Brown Institute been up to?"

"Messing with the process. Somehow they have managed to create stronger genes in, I would guess, a personality? Or traits of some kind? I have been reading up on this. It's almost as if they have mimicked some instincts that animals have, like when a puppy knows to bury its food without anyone teaching it."

"Michael is no puppy."

"Sorry, that was a bad example. The Zander fish may be a better one. It doesn't kill for food, just for sport; it just wants to bite the heads off other fish. It is not taught this, when it is born it just wants to kill. That's what they have done with humans. They have been able to make them murderous or psychopathic, or in Maria's case more compassionate and loyal. I think they are installing emotions before someone is born and those emotions are then prominent in the person."

"There is nothing wrong with Maria." Christopher did not like the thought that Maria would have anything similar to her brother running around inside her. He pulled Maria closer into him.

"I was not saying that, but her file states that they also added this into her."

Christopher sat back. "You gave me their files, Detective? Did you not? There was nothing written in there?"

"The code is small; unless you are looking for it you wouldn't know what it meant. So on their own the files are pretty useless. But as I said before we now have a hard drive."

"And you know everything now?"

"I know a lot."

Christopher looked more uneasy than upset now. There was something about the way that he was looking at Alex she didn't like.

"Where is this hard drive now, Detective?"

Alex was not about to hand the hard drive over to him. Her thoughts suddenly went to a Mellor cover up and the affidavit he made her sign before.

"Back at the station."

"I want him home, Detective. If he has been infected or he is sick I still want him home. I will take care of him at home where he is loved."

Alex knew that he would, this wasn't a father hearing something new about his child. He already knew what Michael was. There was a pause, as if he was ensuring Alex knew what he meant by that.

"What have you done with Harry?" Maria looked up long enough from burying her head in her father's chest just to say those words.

"He is wrapped and on the balcony, there is a lot of blood in this apartment. I had tried to clean the bulk of it up, but if someone comes looking I am not sure that you would be able to clean it all."

Christopher beckoned to one of the men and they checked outside. Alex was getting nervous; she didn't like her odds in this room, as if Christopher really wanted to cover everything up – was he going to take care of her also?

"Tell me where Michael is now?" Christopher was looking directly at another of the guys, who then disappeared out of the apartment.

"I am sure he won't hang around, he brought me here and he knows I am looking for him."

"I am sure he won't, Detective." Christopher pulled Maria's head out of his chest.

"Maria, could you please go and fetch me a bottle of water from downstairs? There is a little shop on the corner. I want to have a word with the detective."

Maria got straight up. She didn't question her father, he had given her the look as if to say, this doesn't concern you. She headed to the door.

"Give me ten minutes."

Alex thought, this is it, with Maria out of the room. They could just as easily make two bodies disappear as they could one. She stood up from the sofa she had been sitting on.

"Sit down, Detective." It wasn't a request, but she didn't sit down either. Two of the men were by the door and Christopher was sitting on the sofa opposite her.

The door opened and the third man came in with a black case, and opened it in front of Christopher. Alex couldn't see the contents but all her thoughts were that it was big enough to hide a gun with a silencer on in it. Christopher pulled out his hand and placed it into the case. There was a beep.

The laptop inside the case had needed a thumb print from Christopher to open. And as it did, he looked at the screen and turned it towards Alex. "He has just landed in England, Detective."

Alex looked at the screen, it was a map of the world and there were three flashing dots on the screen. One was in the USA, one in Italy and the other in England. "You have your family tracked?"

"We are a very rich family, Detective; with over two hundred billion in the bank it makes us a target for every criminal out there. The children do not know hence I asked Maria to leave the room."

"So he has made it to England. Why would he go there? Do you have a house in London?"

"No, Detective, we don't. In fact I believe we have only ever been there once and it rained all the time. Can I ask something of you now? Can you find him? Can you help me clean this up?"

Alex thought before she answered. Is he really asking for him to come back now that Maria is no longer in the room? He has a squad of men ready to do his every bidding, they can find him in a heartbeat? Or is this a fact that should he die or be captured it is probably best for him. Christopher loved his family but Michael was now a huge burden for all three of them.

"Somebody needs to stop him, Detective, for his own good."

That was a clearer sign from him. He didn't want Michael back, he wanted rid of him.

"Take my plane, and keep it till you have things sorted." Christopher nodded again at the third man who produced out of his holdall a stack of euros, about twenty thousand, and handed it to Alex.

"There is more money on the plane should you need it, I want this taken care of, Detective. We will clear up everything that has gone on here."

Alex couldn't stop thinking that she was being asked to be the hired gun now. Money, plane and make sure you take care of him, is what Christopher had said to her.

"I am not sure."

Before she could finish the sentence, Christopher spoke over her. "Detective, as I said, I don't have family or a home in England. There are about seven hundred flights out of Leonardo Airport every day; he is going to England for a reason. I know my son, Detective, when he is backed into a corner he will be blaming someone else for this mess."

Alex had seen first-hand his tantrums, he didn't like to lose and Michael was still a child at heart. But still she didn't want to become Christopher's lapdog. Clearing up the situation with Deacon James had to be done, nobody else knew that it was him so that had to be a job for Alex. Nobody had offered her a stack of cash and a plane to clear it up. Christopher could see that she was contemplating her options.

"Do you have anyone you care about in England, Alex? Anyone who would be close to, say, London Luton Airport?"

Alex finally got it. Christopher had been doing his homework also. He knew that Alex had been to London Luton Airport before. The only other time she had been out of the country before this case was a holiday to Paul's parents with Sophie. It was where she had met Mike. Christopher knew this and so did Michael.

Michael was in England and heading to Paul's parents.

"He is blaming me!"

"As I said, Detective, he will project the fault onto someone else and he seems to have fixated on you? And you have indeed fuelled the fire by coming here. And telling him about his birth place."

Christopher had been having Alex looked into. It was actually he who shared the information with Michael in the first place to try to persuade him a week or so after the stabbing to watch his back. He wanted to point out to Michael that this detective had nothing to lose so he had to be careful. The Mellors had a private detective following her, up until the point of the morning she met Deacon James. Christopher called them off as Michael and Maria were both safe and home and packing for the flight to Rome. There was no need to know what the detective was doing if they were about to leave the country.

"If you need anything at all take this phone." Christopher was now confident she would want to go. She couldn't run the risk of leaving Michael in England with Paul's family. One of the guys handed over his phone. All of Christopher's aids had been issued with burner phones which were changed monthly. Christopher didn't want his movements overheard or tracked by anyone.

"One of my guys will pick up and arrange anything, and I mean anything."

Alex took the phone looking straight at Christopher.

"Take care of this for me, Miss Keaton, and I will ensure you have anything you ever need."

Maria walked back into the apartment, it had been fifteen minutes just to be safe, and handed her dad the water.

"Thanks, dear, Alex is going to help us find Michael and bring him home, isn't that right Alex?"

"Yes."

"Thank you." Maria hugged Alex for the second time. Alex then headed for the door.

"I will ring ahead to the plane, Detective, and it will be waiting to take you wherever you need to go."

Alex glanced back at them and then left. In the last hours she had added bribery, corruption and failure to report a murder to the long list of misdemeanours that she was developing. Alex stood in the hallway after she closed the door wondering what had just happened to her. She was no longer a detective, she was more a criminal than she was a policewoman.

Paul would have been so disappointed with her. Her father, her mother, her brother, all of them wouldn't understand what she was trying to do. But what she could do was stop Michael before he hurt anyone else; at least she hoped she could as he already had half a day on her.

Alex headed back to the hotel and picked up the rest of her stuff. She then got into a cab to the airport. During the sixteen mile drive, Christopher had rung ahead and readied the plane for her. On her arrival she was ushered straight through customs and sitting back on the same plane that a month ago had taken her to Germany and to the Brown Institute. Her life was totally different now.

Whilst taking off she sat staring at the luxury around her, a private jet, champagne on ice. How had the Quaid case brought her to this point?

If she had taken the time to look out of the window at the time she would have been able to make out a fire about ten to fifteen minutes' walk from Vatican City. A small but expensive penthouse apartment had gone up in flames.

By the time she landed in London Luton two hours later the apartment was gone. Christopher and Maria had chartered another plane back home and Harry was at the bottom of the Tevere River, weighted down so heavily that he was never coming back up.

Chapter 11

On arrival at the airport, the captain of the plane came out of the cockpit and went to a safe at the back of the plane. He handed Alex another bundle of money, this time in English pound notes. He didn't say anything to her, just handed the money and went back to his seat. Again she was fast tracked through customs and then given a hire car as she arrived at the other side of the airport.

Alex had been here once before, but never driven here, on the wrong side of the road. She knew Mike lived closer than his parents as they had visited him first on their trip. But she had no idea how to get there or what the address was. Milton Keynes was all she could remember as it was twenty to twenty-five minutes from the airport. Paul's parents were a further fifteen miles away in a little village just off the M1 motorway. Not knowing either of the addresses Alex wasn't sure how she was going to get to them. Michael was here somewhere and she started to believe that he knew more about her than she did herself at the moment.

She texted Mike to say she wanted to send some condolence cards to his mum and dad and maybe him also, not wanting to spook him or them until she met them face to face. It was nine thirty p.m., twenty-five and a half hours since she met Michael in the Coliseum and so much had happened. All she could think of was to start driving.

Heading out of the airport she programmed the sat nav for Milton Keynes. The sat nav had taken her onto the M1, she remembered the road because Paul had been giving her a history lesson on England when she arrived. It had been the first full length motorway in the UK although not the first motorway, there had been a section opened in Preston before 1959. The whole trip was full of useless facts about the UK. But it had been her first trip outside the US, and Paul and Sophie were making it memorable. She was so thankful of that now, as these titbits had stuck in her head.

Alex half remembered the junctions also, the first part of the M1 opened from Watford to Rugby, Paul's football team and his favourite sport. Both his brother and parents lived in this stretch of motorway also, Mike Junction 14 and his parents Junction 16.

Alex pulled into the service station just after Junction 11. She was in the car but she didn't know where she was heading. Milton Keynes was a big place. She tried Mike's phone, but nothing. This was worrying her. She looked through her phone and she had a land line number for Paul's parents. She tried it and got a dead tone at the end of the phone. Something was up. She could feel it.

Alex sat trying to think of all the stupid things that Paul had talked about in his car journey. Milton Keynes was a manmade town. Roundabouts everywhere. That's what she remembered. There were at least a dozen roundabouts after Junction 14 as they came off the motorway, famous for roundabouts and concrete cows, that is what Paul had said. Alex was never going to find Mike's house without an address. Paul's parents' was somewhere to do with a stream. A little village named after a stream. Alex picked up her phone and typed 'stream' into Google, clicked Wikipedia and there were words associated with stream. Brook – it was brook, bugbrook because of the bugs that lay across the stream, or at least that is what Paul had told her.

Alex looked at the sat nav, Bugbrooke thirty-five minutes. Just as she programmed it in her phone rang. It was a withheld number.

"Mike?"

"Either that was to wind me up, or you were expecting someone else, Detective?"

"Michael."

"That is better. I understand you are now helping my father to get me to come home?"

Maria, Alex knew Maria had already been in contact with Michael. "Maria told you?"

"She is my sister, Detective, we tell each other everything. She was my first call after getting a new phone. I wanted to see that she was okay and that good old Daddy turned up to look after her. Imagine my surprise when I found out so had you. Are you not a detective any more, Alex?"

That was a good question to ask, Alex didn't know any more. Her actions over the last few days were more of a vigilante than a detective.

"I mean helping wrap a body up. I am sure that is against the law."

Alex didn't answer his question. She needed to push past this conversation and find out where he was. "Where are you, Michael?"

"Now, now, Detective, you didn't answer my question? Seems to be our thing, doesn't it? Besides if you are helping my father you already know where I am and I would not be surprised to find you even in the same country."

"I mean, where exactly are you?"

"That's a better question. I am presuming Daddy shared his little tracking secret with you? He thinks I don't know about it. I didn't until a couple of years ago, but every time I went off radar one of his goons would turn up as if from nowhere. Imagine my surprise, Detective, when this time he doesn't send one? Why is that do you think?"

Alex wasn't answering that question either. Because your father would prefer to see you dead than returned is not the thing to say to someone already so far over the edge.

"I will tell you what I think, I think Daddy has had enough of Michael and Harry was his last straw. And do you know what I think, Detective?"

"You think it's all my fault, don't you."

"Damn right it is and that's why I am going to do to you what you have done to me."

There was anger in Michael's voice now. The soft playful voice had disappeared.

"Michael, I didn't do this to you. The Brown Institute has done this to you. I haven't done anything to you other than play your little games."

"No, Detective, you are the one who has set me free, all they did was make me. Like my father. But until you come along I held back from who I really was, but now, now I am going to become all that I can be."

"Where are you, Michael? I will come to you and we can talk about this?"

"You know where I am, Detective."

Those words made Alex's heart sink. I do know where you are headed, and I am hoping that you aren't there already, either Mike's house or Mike's parents' house.

"Of a by the way Alex, and as a welcome to England, your lover, Mike, he wasn't home."

The phone went dead. Michael was at Mike and Paul's parents' house. Alex got back on the motorway and headed north. Michael's question kept running through her head. Are you a detective now? Surely she should phone the police and get them to Paul and Mike's parents' house. But if she did wasn't that going to create questions everywhere? It was only yesterday morning when the captain told her to take two weeks off. Since then she had been to Italy and now England. Chasing down someone who you have told the entire force is a murderer and you are going to get him. Alex couldn't think straight, she didn't know who or what she had told people. Her main aim was to get there and save them. But even now she wasn't sure where in this village they lived. She had remembered the name, but the only other thing she could remember was the walk through the village for a Sunday dinner in the local pub, past the little store, a telephone box, through the cemetery to a pub called The Five Bells. That was it, The Five Bells, Paul's dad drank in there every lunchtime. They would know the address.

Alex was off the motorway in thirty minutes and heading towards the town centre. She had remembered Paul talking about the signposts on the way to Harpole, where he used to play football. Right at the roundabout and over a little bridge and they were in Kislingbury. Paul had shared his first kiss with a girl from there called Sarah French. Mike had still teased him up until the day he died about this: a Frenchie in Kissingbury. Alex had remembered all this but she still couldn't remember the house or where it was. She followed the main road through the village until on the right hand side the pub appeared.

Alex ran into the bar, and then froze. What was she going to say to the people there? It wasn't as if she could just shout out 'there is a murderer on the loose and he is looking for John and Claire Simpson'. But she didn't have time to lose.

Approaching the bar, she beckoned over the barmaid. A tall dark beautiful girl, who spoke with a bit of a foreign accent. "Hi, can I help you? We are just about to call last orders."

"Yes, please, I have a package for John Simpson? But the address is a little smudged I could only make out the village?"

"A bit late to be delivering packages, isn't it?"

"I know, it's from his son Mike and I promised I was going to drop it off yesterday and I forgot."

This put the barmaid at ease. She knew Mike as he drank in the pub most Sundays with his father.

"Oh okay, it's 42, I think, Callington Lane. Can't miss it, it's the last house on the left before you get to the new estate. Knowing John though he will have been in bed a couple of hours. He is an early bird."

"Sorry, which is?"

"Top of the road, turn right, past The Bakers Arms, past the little store and at the pet shop, third left, second right, end of the road."

"Thanks."

Alex turned and was out of the door. She followed the woman's instructions. Once she started she remembered the road, and the number. And the fact that it was the last big house on the left. Why had she wasted that time? What if that time was going to cost her?

Alex pulled outside the house. It was in darkness.

The front garden had several trees and a red mini in the driveway. There were no lights on other than the lamp post on the street under which Alex was parked.

Alex got out of her car and headed into the driveway, gun already out just in case, but it was by her side so as not to scare them if they were sitting in and watching television. As she walked up to the garage door she could just about make out that someone had smashed the glass on the security light so it didn't go on and didn't attract attention. She walked up the side of the garage to the front door. Again the security light had been smashed. Michael was here.

Trying the front door, it was locked. Alex had remembered the house as soon as she saw it, to the left of the front door was a walkway and you could get to the back of the house this way. It had a huge garden and John would drive his ride on lawnmower through this passage way to get to the front lawn. Alex headed round the back. The shed to the left of the house light was on. The padlock had been broken and it gave some light to the back of the house. Michael wasn't as careful here, he didn't need to be. The whole garden had been tree-lined and nobody was close enough to see any comings and goings. Alex tried the patio doors to the back and they were open. Entering the house, she had the same feeling as she did at Jack's house a month ago. The feeling that something was wrong here came over her. The patio doors were part of the summer room. Alex headed straight through to the dining room. To the left of her a living room, and to the right an office and a study, all in darkness. Straight on from the dining room was the kitchen and conservatory also still in darkness.

Alex headed quietly up the stairs that lead from the hallway, all the time thinking they may just be asleep, with the thought also in the back of her head of catching Michael in the act.

At the top of the stairs there were five doors, she had remembered staying in the guest room at the bottom of the hallway, Paul's room was next to it and Mike's was in front of her. To her left was the bathroom, to the right was their parents' bedroom. The door was slightly open. She headed over and pushed the door.

She was too late. Even in the darkness she could see the two bodies sprawled across the bed. She stood at the doorway, not wanting to move, not wanting to cry, just numb. She had brought this on them. They were innocent of everything. She had unleashed Michael the murderer to be all that he could be.

She didn't want to but she pulled down her coat over her hand and turned the light on. The blood was everywhere. Jack had shot himself with a gun and there was less blood than what was splattered all over the walls, the bed, the furniture in the room.

Michael had disabled the security lights and gone round the back as Alex had thought. It was Paul's dad who had left the light on in the shed and Michael could see straight in there. There were saws and hammers and drills all hung up, as he used it for a workshop. Michael took one of the hammers from the shed. The patio doors were also open. They were always forgetting to lock them of a night as they would wander in and out of the garden all day.

Michael didn't creep up the stairs like Alex. He had just run straight up them. John was out of the bed already when Michael got to the door, one blow with the hammer across the forehead knocked him to the ground. Claire had started to scream. Michael almost leapfrogged John to get a hit across her head also, she was dead within seconds. Michael picked up John and put him onto the bed. What happened next was twenty years of suppression all coming out in one go. Each body had at least fifty blows to it with full pressure. The blood soaked into every corner of the bed. Michael had been covered head to toe. He then calmly took a shower, grabbed some clothes from John's wardrobe and headed back out.

Michael had been long gone before the call to Alex; she was never going to be able to save them. Alex could see by how the blood was drying that this was done a couple of hours ago. Michael had disabled the security lights as a precaution, not as a necessity. She was fixated on the bed for about five minutes. She could not get the image out of her brain. That was until she looked up at the wall behind them. Written in blood, 'You did this, Alex'.

Michael had written her a message, but not just for her, this way everyone was going to see this. She couldn't just wrap these bodies up and get rid of them. The whole house was covered in blood.

Alex began to realise what she had done. She had also announced to the village she was here. There were at least fifteen people in the bar earlier and as an outsider they all got a good look at her. Her car was parked under the street light outside. Anyone still up would have got a look at this and a look at Alex creeping up the pathway and round the back of the house. Alex was still struggling to realise who she was, but she did know who she wasn't, she wasn't a very good murderer or criminal. What if Michael had set her up, for all she knew the police were en route this very minute? She needed to get out. She stood staring at the message on the wall wondering whether she should wipe it off. If she did her DNA would be here, she wasn't sure that she would get away with it. There are a lot of Alexs in the world and it was a unisex name – they weren't going to put one with the other straight away. And she needed to find Mike to ensure that Michael didn't do the same to him.

Alex turned off the light to the bedroom. This wasn't how she wanted to see Paul's parents again so on the way down the hall she stopped and looked at a picture of them with Paul and Mike. She wanted a different last image of them. It didn't work. Alex went back the way she came and ensured she kept her head bowed down getting into the car. She needed to get some distance from the house and the village but also head towards Mike. She tried his phone again but there was no answer. Alex found the motorway again and drove down to Junction 13, close enough to Milton Keynes to see if she could get hold of Mike.

There was a hotel about a mile off the road and Alex booked herself in as Sophie Mellor. She paid cash so no questions were asked. On the way to the room she got two bottles of water and some chocolate from the vending machine. There had been no food or drink available as it was too late, but her stomach was still churning from the images at the house so water was going to be all that she could manage.

She needed another shower. She needed to get the smell of blood away. Alex stood under the water for twenty minutes. Everything was running through her head. Everything from Jack Quaid, to where she had arrived at today. She had managed to kill or get killed most of Paul's family and for all she knew Mike was already dead. She had been a witness to several murders and now a contract hire killer for the Mellors. Whilst all this was still running through her head she still believed that every action she had taken had been for the right reasons. She wasn't a criminal. The work she was doing was necessary. There was a chance that all of these people were going to become Stephen McAndrews or Deacon James; the captain had said that Deacon James could have been the biggest serial killer in history. And her actions had led to his capture. Well, her actions led to his death and the end to the killing. So that must have counted for something.

Alex got out of the shower and opened her go bag. The bottle of champagne that Michael had left in the room of the hotel was still in there. She wasn't really sure why she took it when she packed. For a brief moment she had thought that when this was all over she could sit back and drink it. Given the hard drive had thousands of names on it, she knew deep down this was never going to be over.

She ignored the bottle and pulled out a top. It had been Paul's T-shirt, a spare one from his locker. When she cleared it out for Sophie after he had died she kept it for herself. She put it on when she was really low and it somehow brought her closer to him. She put it on now, but there was a guilt associated with what she was doing. She had loved him so much, but she couldn't help but think about what she was doing to his family now. What her actions had led too.

The phone rang. Alex picked it up and was afraid to speak first.

"Hi." It was Michael.

Alex didn't reply.

"Are you not speaking to me now, Alex?"

"Where are you, Michael?"

"Oh you are speaking to me, good. I am close, Detective; I guess I should start calling you something else as I didn't see any blue lights at the house when you left?"

Michael was still there. He had been watching her go through all of that. Alex's blood began to boil. "You were still there?"

"I was close, Detective, sorry Alex. I thought you would have called for backup? But it seems you sneaked away and left them. Doesn't that make you an accessory now?"

It did, at least it made her in the failure to report category. She knew she was probably now number one suspect.

"You should have come and said hi." The tone of Alex's voice told Michael what he really meant.

"I guess you are one of my father's goons, now. How much did he pay you to come and get me?"

"Nothing."

Alex thought about it, he did pay her, he gave her twenty thousand euros and he had witnesses. The captain of the plane also gave her money out of the box and you can guarantee that plane had a camera showing it happen.

"I know my father, he will have given you something. He is a devious one that one. Once you are in his pocket, Alex, you are there for life. So did you get my message?"

Michael knew that she had. It wasn't as if she was going to miss it, this was his way of just trying to draw her in.

"It will not be long before they are looking into who is the nearest 'Alex' to the family. Hell, there are pictures of you downstairs in the living room, Alex. They will put two and two together and get five at this rate."

Alex knew this was true. She didn't know when, but at some point she was going to get the call to answer some questions on the killing.

"Michael, we need to end this before it gets out of hand."

"Gets out of hand?" Michael raised his voice. "Gets out of hand, Alex, we haven't even started yet. You and I, we are going on a journey, Alex. You have started something that we are going to finish. Once I have taken out everyone that you care about."

Alex believed him. She believed that he was ready to take them all, her father, mother, brother and his family. Michael had the taste now, there was going to be no stopping him. Alex didn't want to mention them. She left a pause to see what was coming next. Nothing was.

"And Mike?" Alex didn't want to know the answer but she had to ask the question. Was it too late for that also?

"Ah yes, the one night stand, he is missing and Alex, I have to say I have been looking."

Mike was still alive, but with Michael on his case, how long for?

"He has nothing to do with this, Michael. This is you and me, and the Brown Institute. Go after them. I will help you."

Michael was silent. He did blame them, and his father and his mother, but at the moment his fixation was with Alex.

"Good night, Detective, I mean, Alex. Sweet dreams."

Michael hung up the phone. Alex rang Mike's number again, straight through to voicemail again. This time she left a message, told him she was in England and to call her straightaway. She didn't leave a name, or a number for fear that someone else may get to his phone before she did.

Alex lay on the bed. There was little else she was going to do tonight. Mike was somewhere and Michael hadn't got to him which was the main thing.

Tomorrow someone was going to find the Simpsons, and Michael's message. It wasn't going to be long before someone was coming looking for Alex. Michael was right, there were holiday pictures of her downstairs and her at the fiftieth birthday party in London. She knew she would be the first port of call. But the best thing she could do for herself and for Mike now was rest. She needed to be ready for the day ahead and the challenge of finding Michael and dealing with him. Alex pulled the covers over her and turned off the light.

Chapter 12

Alex was sleeping heavily and woke to the phone ringing. "Alex?" it was Mike. Alex was so overwhelmed to hear his voice. At the same time she was stumped with what to say to him. Your parents have been murdered by a psychopath and he is looking for you, wasn't the way she needed to handle him.

"Alex?"

"Sorry. So glad to hear your voice. I have just woke up."

"I have just got your message. You are here in England?"

"Yes I am, where are you, Mike?"

"I am in London, having breakfast and then heading back home. I was at a work's dinner last night and there was no reception in the hotel. So I missed all your calls."

"Mike, don't go to home. It is not safe, I need to see you."

"Alex, what is so important that you have travelled halfway around the world to talk to me about?"

"I can't explain on the phone, whereabouts in London are you?"

"Camden Town, it's on the Northern Line if you are by a tube station?"

"Okay, I will find it and call you when I am close."

"If you come out of the tube station, cross the road and take the first right, I am about five minutes up from there, in a bar called The

Earl of Camden. I am meeting some people there for breakfast. I can wait for you afterwards if you like?"

"I will be an hour and a half, at the most."

Alex knew London wasn't far as on her last visit they had got the train from Northampton to London for Paul's uncle's party which took less than an hour and she was already down the M1.

"Okay, I will wait. Are you okay, Alex?"

"I will be, I just need to see you, be safe." Alex hung up the phone. Mike was alive and more importantly nowhere near Michael, she hoped.

Alex dressed as quickly as she could, and headed out of the hotel and back onto the M1. She remembered Paul saying not to drive into London as you can never get out, the last thing she wanted was to be stuck in a car with a mad man chasing her. Alex headed to Watford and got the train into Euston. Camden was a short hop on the tube from there. Alex was in London in less than an hour and a quarter. She headed towards the bar that Mike had mentioned and could see him through the window. He was sitting with three other guys and they were just finishing up as they were paying the bill. Alex waited for them to leave and then came in.

"Alex."

"Mike."

"I did mean to call after the other night, honest, you don't have to stalk me all the way back to England."

"It's not that." Alex started to cry, the crying quickly turned into sobbing. Everything she had seen in the last twenty-four hours hit her like a brick wall. Harry, Mike's parents, so much blood, so much violence. Even for a police officer it was too much.

"Hey, come on, sit down."

Mike got up and pulled her close to him sitting her on the bench next to him. It took Alex five minutes to compose herself so that she could speak again.

"What has happened?"

The lies that were stacking up in Alex's mind needed some order. But she also needed him to be safe from the truth.

"I went back over what we discussed the other day at the funeral, when you said that you couldn't get over the fact that this wasn't tied to the Ducasse case that took Paul away from us, and I found a link."

Michael sat back a little from Alex. "What kind of link?"

"The worst kind, it would seem that it had been revenge for one of the mobsters that was taken down in the hit. A rogue hitman if you like, operating all by himself."

"And you came all this way to tell me that? It is good news, Alex, but we could have discussed it on the phone."

"No, you don't understand, I tracked the guy to England, he flew into Luton last night and I understand he is coming for you."

"For me?"

"Yes for you. He believes Paul shot his brother. And he wants revenge against you."

Alex was lying through her teeth so much now with ease. Less than a month ago she was in the clinic in Germany with Chris where she couldn't get a lie out of her mouth. Now she couldn't even remember the truth. Mike sat back on the bench. He didn't know what to make of the information. As he did, across the road by the lamp post was Michael. In broad daylight, he had a hooded top on but he raised his hand to acknowledge her. She had led Michael directly to Mike. He didn't know where he was, Michael must have been close to the hotel last night so that he could follow Alex this morning. The fact was

Michael was in the hotel last night about four doors to the right of Alex. As she checked out Michael had gone down the back stairs and was already in his car waiting when she left. Alex hadn't thought about this again. She sat looking at him, Mike leaned forward again.

"And did Paul kill his brother?"

Alex tried to look behind Mike, but Michael was gone. Alex sat back, even she knew he wasn't going to do anything in a crowded bar, but she wasn't comfortable sitting there.

"No, there was only one guy left when we went in and I shot him."

"So why doesn't he think you did it?"

"I think he does, I think I am on his list also."

Alex knew she was on Michael's list but not now, he wanted her to suffer as much as possible. Michael knew that when he returned to America though he would have to deal with his father. And doing so wouldn't be as easy as playing with Alex.

"Where is he now?"

"I don't know, all we know is he is looking for you." Alex had lied, she didn't want to spook him into doing anything rash like calling the police, and telling him Michael was across the street would have done that.

Mike started to become uneasy. "So do we need to call the police, get some protective custody going on?"

"Not really, we don't know what he looks like, or who he is, other than he is here for revenge on you? Not a lot to go on really."

"So, someone is coming to kill me, we don't know who, when, or how? How do we even know this is true?"

Alex was trying to work out an answer in her head before speaking.

Michael sat in the coffee shop across the road. He could see Alex and Mike talking from where he was. He hadn't intended on waving to her but it was just a knee jerk reaction. Michael was intrigued by what Alex was going to say to Mike. Clearly she couldn't tell him about his parents as he would have been up and out of there by now. In fact when was anyone going to find out about his parents? Michael didn't know them and it could be days before they found the bodies; that wasn't any fun. Michael picked up his phone. He dialled 999.

"Hello, police. I am worried about my parents. I can't seem to get hold of them on their phone or their mobiles which is so unusual. I have rung the neighbours and they have said that they haven't seen them all morning. I am so worried."

"Okay sir, can you give me the address and I will ensure someone drops round to see them."

"Yes it's 42 Callington Lane, Bugbrooke, Northampton. Thank you and if you can hurry, I am so worried." Michael hung up the phone and sat back in his chair, smiling as he did it, still with one eye on the two of them chatting.

"He called me."

"The killer?"

"Yes, that's how I know he was targeting you." It wasn't a lie; the killer had been calling her. What she didn't say was that it was her he was targeting, this was all because of her, what she had been doing. She didn't want to say, I am the reason, Paul, Sophie, your parents are all dead, it's all me. Alex still carried around with her the guilt from the shooting at the hotel where Paul had died. She just felt that if she did something different, stopped him barging in, if she had made him wear his vest when he should have, Paul would still have been alive today and none of this would be happening.

Now Mike was the only family Paul would have had left and she needed to protect him.

"I would suggest we just get out of here, somewhere where there aren't as many windows, as there are just too many angles to look for."

Mike grabbed his jacket and followed Alex out of the bar. Michael was still in the coffee shop watching as they walked down the street and to the left. He followed.

"Where do you want to go?"

"I am not sure but I just have a feeling he is close and we need to lose him first of all." This made Mike nervous, especially when he could see Alex was continually looking around for someone. Alex knew Michael was here and he wouldn't go far, she had Mike and he was coming for him.

"The horse market is down there, it's always packed with people. You could lose anyone in there."

"That will do."

Alex and Mike walked with pace the five-minute walk to the entrance of the Old horse market. Alex was so focused she didn't even see the number of tattoo parlours and burlesque shops that adorned Camden High Street. Normally, being a young quiet shyly brought up girl this type of place would really interest her. As they entered the horse market stalls full of food, Chinese, Indian, pizza were at every turn. Followed by stalls selling old records and ladies' clothing, all manner of weird and wonderful things were on sale here. Most of all the market was like a rabbit warren, little side streets turning off everywhere, you could turn a corner and end up anywhere. And for about twenty minutes they did just that, until they were confident that nobody was following them.

Michael wasn't, he had tried and lost them in the market place. He turned back towards the tube station and parked himself in a restaurant so that he could see the comings and goings of the people getting the tube.

Alex stopped to think of her next move. What would she do, not as a detective but as a stalker, cut them off at the source? She knew he would go back to the tube so they needed to do something different. Alex headed out of the market and jumped into the nearest cab.

"Where to?"

Alex looked at Michael for an answer.

"I don't know, St Pancras?"

"St Pancras, it is." The taxi driver started to move.

"Why didn't we just get back on the tube?"

"Because that's where I would have been waiting for us. If he was there and been following me that is where I would wait."

It took about thirty minutes in traffic to get to the station. After paying the driver Alex took Michael inside the building and to the nearest coffee shop. They ordered coffee and sat down.

"I still can't believe this is all happening."

Mike's phone rang, it was work and he had received a call from the police. And they were asking for him to call them back.

"That's from me, I was frantically looking for you last night and reported you missing." Alex didn't want Mike to find out about his parents just yet as if he did it was almost certainly going to get messy with the police.

"I think you should turn your phone off."

"Why?"

"Because, if he can get your number from work, he can trace it. You can almost get an app to do that nowadays."

Mike turned his phone off, just as Alex's phone rang. She placed it on the table and put it on speaker phone.

"Michael."

"Hi, Alex, its seems you have started to think like a criminal and not a detective."

"Where are you, Michael?"

"I am outside the tube station in Camden, but you knew that, didn't you? Catch on quick, don't you."

She could see Mike desperate to talk so she grabbed him by the hand.

"As I said, Michael, this is between you and me, we don't need Mike involved in this,"

"He is family, Alex, the lengths you will go to protect your family. Mine have been taken away from me. So an eye for an eye."

Everything that Michael had been saying was backing up the story that she had told, she needed to end the call as quickly as possible, so that she could keep this lie alive.

"As I said, Michael, it's just us, let it be just us."

"As I said, Alex, it's not. Give him my condolences and I will be seeing you both soon." Michael hung up the phone.

"Condolences, why would he be saying that?"

"He means Sophie, he said the same to me the first time he rang." Mike believed her. He had no doubt in his mind that Michael was coming for him or any indication that his parents were dead.

The police had arrived at the Simpson house and entered the house the same way that Alex and Michael had. They went upstairs and found the room just as Alex had.

Within thirty minutes there were a dozen cars outside and a bunch of onlookers from the street, including the barmaid from The Five

Bells. She lived on the same street and spoke to the policemen about a young woman calling in last night looking for the address with some kind of package. They had recently installed a camera into the bar area as the owners had moved out of the flat upstairs and into a house down the road. One of the policemen followed her back to the bar. Within an hour they had the name and description of the number one suspect. Detective Alex Keaton.

"I am not sure what we should do now."

"I still think the police are our best bet, but if all we have is a name it's not going to be a good plan."

"No, we need to capture him and take him in, he has already confessed to me about Sophie's murder, we need him on tape doing that and then we can arrest him. I don't have any pull over here, I am just a tourist and jumped onto a plane to come and see you to make sure you are safe. I haven't even spoken to my captain about this. I know this is a lot to ask you, Mike. But you and I are the bait we need to catch the guy, he and his family are responsible for Paul and Sophie. And we are the only people that can do something about it." Alex needed to highlight that they were all alone in this. There was nowhere for them to go for help. And if this was going to work they were going to have to do it alone and together to catch a hitman.

"My uncle, the one whose party you came to, he has a place down in Cornwall. Its only small and it's a cabin in the woods basically; we could go there? I am sure I could set something up with regards to a camera to get a confession out of him."

Mike was starting to think like a detective. Alex was starting to think like a murderer. If she was going to get Michael she was going to have to kill him or else he wouldn't stop. And someone with that much money could carry on from inside prison if he wanted to. A remote cabin in the woods would be a perfect place to be able to take care of Michael.

"Sounds perfect. I have a car at Watford station. We can use this, how far is Cornwall?"

"It's a good five hours at least and we will need to stop for supplies somewhere. Alex, your phone. We don't want him surprising us, we want to be traced when we need to be."

Alex knew that Michael wasn't tracing the phones but she couldn't risk anyone contacting Mike about his parents. She turned off her phone.

They both boarded a train to Euston and then to Watford. Picking up the car and heading round the M25 to the M4, they stopped at the Patchway at Bristol for supplies. They were going to need food and drink and cameras of some description. Mike pointed out they were commonplace now – they were even selling them in Asda for webcams. Michael had a laptop and could stream the confession online. Alex didn't tell him she had no plan to get a confession out of Michael. She did intend to kill him and get as far away as possible from the body. A cabin in the woods sounded perfect for this. It was still a drive down the M5 and the A30 to Cornwall and was ten p.m. before they arrived in the cabin. Mike put the heating on, it was run on oil and wasn't the best. It was too dark to collect the wood from the barn so it was going to have to do for the night. Alex opened a bottle of wine and made some food. They had both had a long day. Mike had a plan to set up cameras in each of the corners of the room which he could Bluetooth directly to his laptop. This was his chance to avenge his brother and his sister-in-law. He didn't want Michael to get away with this.

Two glasses of wine later they both retired to separate rooms. The last time they had met had ended with them sharing a bed but not tonight. Both of them were too tired for that. Alex needed to sleep and she couldn't really face the guilt of knowing what had happened to his parents and keeping this from him. This was for the best. Separate rooms for the evening. They were safe and tomorrow they were going to have to find a way to capture Michael.

Chapter 13

Alex was cold. The heating clearly hadn't been on in the cabin for quite some time and was struggling to get going again. She almost wished they had gone looking for firewood last night. It was three a.m. and she was wide awake. They had only gone to bed at midnight but she couldn't sleep. The wine had helped but she kept dreaming of Paul and Mike's parents and the fact that at some point Mike was going to find out. She lay in the bed contemplating her actions over the last few days and what her actions were going to be going forward. Could she return to work as if none of this ever happened? She had the hard drive in her bag which was going to lead her to the next murderer and then the next one. She couldn't hop all over the world solving crimes. People were going to notice this.

It was no good, she wasn't sleeping and she was freezing. As much as she didn't mean it sexually maybe some body heat would change that. She stepped out of her bed and put on a robe that was on the back of the door. She headed down the corridor and into the room that Mike had taken. Without saying a word she dropped the robe and cuddled up behind him. He was cold also she could tell, she wrapped her arms around him. He was really cold and really wet. As Alex pulled back her hand she smelled the blood long before she saw it.

"Think it was a one night thing, Alex. I don't believe he is looking for any company in there?"

The light went on, and Alex jumped out of the bed. She was naked, she and the bed were both covered in blood. Mike hadn't moved.

Michael was standing in the doorway with Alex's gun. It was over.

"What? What have you done?" Alex knew what he had done, she just couldn't deal with it. "How did you know we were even here?"

"Because I followed you, Alex. Put the dressing gown on if you like." Michael nodded towards the robe on the floor. Alex did like. It was one thing to be here with Michael now, with your own gun pointing at you. But it was another to do so completely naked.

"You didn't have to kill him, Michael, I told you that."

"Oh, but I did, Alex. I told you I would and I am a man of my promises."

"So you lied? You lied about being at the tube station back in London."

"No, it wasn't a lie, Alex, I was there. Okay, I wasn't there when I was talking to you but I was there waiting to see if you would come back and get back on the train to Watford. I followed you from the hotel to Watford station, Alex. It was a long shot, and losing me in the market was a clever idea. I was almost certain you wouldn't come back for your car."

So stupid. Alex felt so stupid, why hadn't she thought of that? Why didn't she connect that that was going to be the next thing that he did. Mike was dead because of her, the whole family wiped out because of her.

"So what now, Michael? Just going to kill me and get it over with?"

"What now, Alex, is we go into the living room and have a chat." Michael moved to one side and pointed at the door for Alex to go through. As Alex walked closer to the door her thought was to spring at him, but the gun was pointed directly at her, she knew he wouldn't think twice about killing her.

Alex walked over to the table.

"Before we start, it has been playing on my mind, how do you feel?"

"What?"

"How do you feel, Alex, how do you feel about not being Alex the detective any more? And now that you are Alex the criminal, Alex the murderer?"

"I am not a murderer."

"Oh but you are, Alex, if you haven't seen the news then there is a picture of you all over it. I can't believe you actually stopped in the pub to get directions to the house? Alex, I couldn't have written that any better."

The drive to the cabin from London had taken about seven to eight hours and all they did was talk on the way down. They hadn't even put the radio on. Alex had been purposely avoiding anything that might inform Mike what was going on.

"I followed you here and sat just far enough away so that you couldn't see me. When I saw you going to be in separate rooms I presumed it was because of the fact that you had told him about his parents."

"Mike didn't know what you had done to his parents."

"Alex, what you have done is more accurate."

"I haven't done anything, Michael."

"This is true, you are correct you are still a person of interest, and let's be fair. I didn't actually clean the scene up, did I? At some point they will link me to this also, I am sure of it."

"You don't seem bothered about that?"

"I am not, those days are over, Alex, it's all about the future now, and I guess we are linked together in that."

Alex made her move and ran towards Michael. Michael just raised the gun and calmly shot at the floor in front of her. She stood still.

"Now, Alex, why did you do that, I was going to play nice. Sit down. Sit down." Michael was insisting now, she sat on one of the dining room chairs. Michael placed the gun to her head with one hand and pulled the cord from the robe out with the other. He then stood behind her and roped her hands together and to the back of the chair. Her hands hurt, he had made sure they were tied so tight. He then came back around in front of her, her robe was half open and there was a moment when she thought he was about to fully open it. He didn't, he pulled it across her and ensured she was at least semi covered up with the robe.

"I do not want you to catch a cold now, do I? That wouldn't be very sporting, would it?"

Alex was thankful of that, she didn't believe he desired her. She wasn't his type and whilst he may want to kill her at some point, she was a plaything for him at the moment. She knew that he wasn't used to being alone and today she was the only person in his life.

"So from the beginning, Alex, we aren't going anywhere until I know everything." Michael sat back in his chair.

Alex told him, she had nothing to lose, if she explained it all. Hopefully it would take all of the focus away from her and her family. She told the story of finding Jack and his obsessions, the McAndrew case, Joseph Manning, everything up until the point of meeting Michael and Maria, continuing with the Brown Institute, how his father had funded the move and didn't even know about it. She left out the part about killing Sophie, but did include the Deacon James' case and where she was when he first rang. She wanted to prove to Michael that there was someone else to blame for this. It wasn't Alex and her family. She even told him about Jack's letter and the hard drive. Michael had it all now, he knew the whole story. Minus a few names, Alex tried to keep names out of the conversation as she didn't want him to make them targets.

"So do you think my dad knew what they were doing or not?"

"He certainly didn't at the time, all he and your mother wanted was just a baby."

"But does he know now?"

"Yes, he knows now, I said that."

"How did he react, Alex?"

That was a good question, Alex didn't see any change in Christopher, and it was all taken in his stride. Surely that wasn't the action of a father who just found out someone had tampered with his children? Did he know already? That was certainly what Michael was hinting at. The thought hadn't until now crossed her mind but it was doing now.

"My dad doesn't give away a hundred million for no reason, I know him. He may look like an old fuddy duddy but I know that when it comes to his money he is very particular in what he uses it for. And he certainly wouldn't give it away without knowing the full history."

The more Alex thought about it the more she was convincing herself that Christopher was part of it. Michael leant forward on his chair looking directly at Alex.

"What now, I wonder?"

He moved his hand inside her robe and rubbed her down her right side. Alex froze. He had her breast in one hand and a gun in the other pointing directly at her head.

"I am just teasing, Alex, now is not the time for this."

Michael stood up and walked across to the kitchen for a glass of water. All the time he was facing that direction Alex was frenetically trying to undo the ropes on the chair.

Michael turned with the water in his hand. "I think we are done, Miss Keaton." He took a sip of water. "I would like to thank you for your time today, it was very informative. To say the least."

"Where are you going, Michael?"

"Now that is the question isn't it, do you know I don't really know myself at the moment? You have just filled my head with so much information. But I will be taking your gun though, never really had a gun, other than the days I used to go shooting with my father"

"Michael, enough people have died over this."

"Alex, no they haven't, you and I both know now that there is a purpose for people like me, hence why would they want to breed us."

Alex couldn't argue with the logic, why had the Brown Institute started this. Just because they could? Look at what they had created, thousands of killers worldwide, and for what? Or was that where Christopher had come into this? Alex had thoughts of contract killers, armies of natural born killers.

"It was a pleasure, Alex, one that we will repeat real soon."

"Don't go, Michael, stay and talk some more."

"People to meet, Miss Keaton. People to meet."

Michael left by the front door. Alex stood up and grabbed the chair, hammering it down on the floor to break. It took five attempts and then it broke. She pulled at the rope with her hands until it came undone. It did, but before she got to the door she could hear the car pulling out of the drive and down the road. Alex opened the door in time to see the headlights disappear into the distance. She stood in the doorway, unsure of what she thought she was going to do if she had caught up with Michael. She was hardly prepared for him in her open dressing gown.

She went back in and closed the door. Michael had gone again, and left murders in his wake. Murders that again could be linked to Alex. Her DNA was all over Mike, so much so she had even had her arms around him and in his blood. She went back to Mike's room just to check that he was really dead. She knew the answer but she wanted a different one. Michael had been more merciful this time, but Alex believed that was because he didn't want to wake her. He wanted to surprise her. He had climbed into the living room window, through the house and into Mike's room without a sound. He cut his throat from ear to ear and by the looks of it held his mouth with his hand as he did. There was a hand shaped impression on Mike's face, from the mud on Michael's gloves.

Alex sat staring at Mike. If she had just done something different, seemed to be Alex's second thought of everyday. If she had just done something different it would have worked out better, but this was fast becoming her world. The only difference she was ever going to make was to stop these people over and over again. She had stopped Deacon James and she could do it again. Alex tucked the covers over Mike. She knew he wasn't going to be cold but she didn't want anyone finding him like that. She then returned to the living room, tied the rope back around her dressing gown and cleared up the mess of the chair. She also cleared away the glasses and the food that they had made and threw them all in the trash. There was no sense making it easy for anyone coming in to identify her. She needed as much time as possible to be able to chase Michael.

Within thirty minutes, Alex was back in the shower. Showering blood off her hands and out of her hair had become a daily occurrence for her. She repacked her bag and clothes and headed out of the cabin. She fully intended to call the police when she was as far away as possible, to tell them about Mike so that someone could come and bury him. That thought made her feel even worse as it would have been someone, just a random person as there was nobody left in his family to grieve for him.

Alex's only thoughts in the car were to get back to the plane. It was still at Luton airport and it was at her beck and call for as long as she needed it. The drive to Luton at that time of the morning took a little over five hours and she arrived into the executive lounge. The pilot was in a hotel close by and she boarded the plane to wait for him. It was going to be a few hours before they would be clear to take off so Alex had a few hours to find Michael.

Alex picked up the phone that one of Christopher's men had given to her.

"Hello, can I speak to Christopher?"

"Christopher is here, Miss Keaton, but I am sure you understand that he cannot speak to you directly?"

"What? What do you mean?"

"He cannot speak to you directly on the account that you are a person of interest in a double murder in England."

"Chasing down his fucking son, I am." Alex was fuming at this. He will know she wasn't responsible.

"I have lost Michael and I need to know where he is."

"Hold on one moment." The phone was quiet, the more this was developing the more Alex believed that Christopher Mellor was involved somewhere along the line. He had played her as well as anyone can. She was more mixed up in this than she could believe.

"It looks like he boarded an early plane out of Bristol airport, which landed in Germany about fifteen minutes ago."

Germany, Alex was thankful that he wasn't halfway across the Atlantic, heading towards her family. She sat back in the chair.

"Mr Mellor wants to know if you will be going to Germany."

Alex thought for a minute, what choice did she have now? It will never be over until Michael is caught or dead. "Yes, I will be going to Germany."

"Miss Keaton, Mr Mellor would like to know if there is anything else you need to carry out his request."

Alex heard the words again – his request – he hadn't actually said in so many words kill my son but she knew that was what was implied for her to do.

After all the things that Michael had done in the past seventy-two hours, Alex didn't feel any remorse for what she had to do, in fact it was now a sense of purpose. He had to die like Sophie had to die, there was no choice about this now.

"I need a gun." There was silence again at the end of the phone.

"The captain will service your needs when he arrives." With that the phone went dead.

Alex was still mad at the thought of Christopher's abandonment of her. But it was going to be a few hours before anything was going to happen so she needed to see if she could relax. She noticed on the side by the kitchen area there was a drinks trolley. Every kind of alcohol she could think of was stored there. She stood up and poured herself a large brandy, almost downed it in one go. She poured another and sat back down, taking this a little slower but still eventually finishing it. Alex relaxed in the chair, Michael was gone, that was the last thought she had before falling asleep.

Michael had arrived in Germany, but it was a big place. Alex had told him about the Brown Institute but not who was running it and who would be the person in charge. She had purposely omitted all the names. Michael had one goal. That was payback for what they had done to him. Michael headed to the Brown Institute and booked into the same hotel that Alex and Jack had stayed in. In his room he started to research the facility, over three thousand people worked at the Brown Institute. He wasn't going to be able to kill all of them. There was a list of board members but no direct leader was published online. The funding had come privately out of donations and Michael was convinced that his father had something to do with this. He wasn't going to get all the information that he needed online, he was going to have to go to the Institute to see if he could get any more information. Besides he was made by these people, surely he had rights.

He phoned them and made an appointment. He told them the truth about who he was and the receptionist looked up his file and there he was on record. It wasn't unusual for people to want to know where and how they were born and requests like these were commonplace. They had a department to deal with this and Michael made a nine a.m. appointment. He was going to have the day to himself. He needed to do something to keep himself occupied.

Chapter 14

Michael had the afternoon to himself. It had been the first time he had time to reflect on the goings on of the last few days. He found a coffee shop opposite the Brown Institute and watched as the people came in and out of the building. At the same time he thought about the direction his life had taken him. There was actually a sense of purpose to him now. All his life he had felt different, he had urges and couldn't understand why nobody else around him had these urges too. His sister, who was his closest friend, was nothing like him. He always used to put it down to being a girl, but he knew that wasn't true. She didn't act or feel the same as he did. There was never any rage or desire to hurt anyone in her eyes, but Michael's had been filled with it from an early age. At the age of ten his father taught him how to shoot on the estate. Just wild game, pigeons, geese, partridges. Michael was a natural and he loved it, his father would ensure that he took him on all his shoots. But Michael was more fascinated by the animal after he had shot it. Michael purposely didn't shoot to kill he always wanted to injure the animal and watch it die. That's what led him to kill the family dogs. He liked to see things suffer. By the age of thirteen Christopher had to stop him from the shoots. He could see what was happening to Michael.

The sense of purpose Michael was feeling, he put down to a release. He felt a release for who he was. He wasn't strange, indifferent, he was exactly who he was meant to be. And if anything his father and mother and sister had been holding him back from this. It all started to make sense now, the visits to the Vatican Museums as kids, all that death and destruction, all of that was part of who he was supposed to grow into.

The people across the road from where he was today had made sure of that. Michael didn't know whether to kill them or kiss them. There was no remorse for what he had done. And if there was then this would be classed as revenge for all the people he had killed. But he didn't feel anything for these people. He was a natural predator and this was the way it was.

Michael's urges to kill were stronger than ever. Four kills in as many days, the taste for blood and the feel of taking life in your hands was powerful, it was a drug habit that needed a fix. But four p.m. in the afternoon in a sleepy coffee shop was not the place to get this. Michael wanted the club atmosphere, he missed his and Maria's club back home. It gave him a sense of power when he was there. Clothes were an issue. He was going to need some. He finished up his coffee and headed closer to the centre of town to look for a clothes shop.

Michael would normally have them handmade but there was no time for that. At the moment all he had were a few pairs of jeans, a couple of tops and one pair of socks. He found a Ralph Lauren store, it was the closest thing to well dressed he was going to find. When he walked in he was greeted by at least three young men all looking him up and down as if he was a fashion victim or Julia Roberts from 'Pretty Woman'.

Two guys stood back and one guy stood forward. Chris, the manager of the store, looked Michael up and down. "Don't we look underdressed, but I can spot Edward Green shoes anywhere."

Michael smiled at him. "They are my gardening shoes."

Chris was thirty, tall, blonde and blue eyed. In Germany he would be classed as the perfect race. And he was exactly the person that Michael was looking for. The other two guys turned and went back to what they were doing behind the counter.

"I need some clothes."

"I can see that, come with me and we can fix you right up."

Michael followed Chris over to the other side of the shop.

"What type of clothes were you thinking about?"

"I need two suits, six shirts, some casual clothes and shoes, maybe three pairs."

"I do like a man that knows what he wants. We don't stock shoes but I can get one of my assistants to run across the road and get you a selection. They are not Edward Green's but there is a Crockett & Jones outlay store there, if you look like James Bond you may as well wear his shoes."

Chris beckoned one of the guys over to him.

"What is your size, sir?"

"Eleven."

Chris smiled at Michael. He then escorted Michael to stand on a box, so he could take his measurements. Chris hadn't needed to take measurements in five years. He had an eye for this type of thing, but he couldn't control himself. He measured Michael in every possible way, gracefully touching his neck, his arms, his inside thigh. Even by Michael's past history he could tell a flirt when he saw one.

Once the measurements were done Chris headed off and came back with a full rack of clothes, a blue suit and a black one, a dozen shirts and three pairs of jeans with six tops. By then the other assistant had returned with a selection of shoes, two black, two brown.

Michael was fixated by Chris's gaze. "I will take them all."

The other assistant spoke up. "Don't you want to try any of them on, sir?"

Michael was now looking directly at Chris. "Are they going to fit me?"

"Perfectly."

That was good enough for Michael. Chris beckoned to both shop assistants to come and wrap up all the clothes.

"If you like, sir, we could have these delivered to your home."

"I am staying in a hotel around the corner. I can walk it from here."

Michael was looking directly at Chris, when he said that.

"That's fine, one of these young men will help you carry those."

Michael handed over his credit card to Chris. It was black, just black with no writing on it. There were only a thousand black cards in the world and it was a status symbol. For the first time Michael thought about money. What if his father had cut him off? What if the card didn't work? Money was something they never worried about and they didn't have separate accounts. Michael's dad had given him and Maria a black card on their twenty-first birthday. There were instructions not to buy a yacht or a car without permission but generally everything else was okay.

The card beeped straight through. Michael was relieved. Michael's father had thought about cancelling his card, but then if anyone ever found out there would be questions why. No, he was now leaving his problem to Alex.

On the back of the receipt Chris was writing something. Michael was pretending not to look as he handed the receipt over to him.

"Have a nice day, sir, and please come again."

Michael took the receipt and the card and put them back in his wallet. It was a short walk back to the hotel and the assistant was carrying most of the clothes. He went to his room and tipped him ten euros after he hung everything in the wardrobe.

Michael closed the door behind him and opened his wallet. He pulled out the receipt. Meet me at Passion eleven p.m. Chris. X. Michael had gone fishing and caught tonight's supper.

The captain woke Alex at four thirty p.m. She had been sleeping for almost five hours. There was no need to wake her earlier as five p.m. was the earliest that they could take off. He handed her a box and some money and went back to the cockpit. He didn't ask any questions. He had been used to that over the last fifteen years in the Mellor service.

Alex opened the box and there was a gun, some ammo and a gun permit for Germany. Who was Christopher Mellor? Alex knew he had money but that was passed down by his parents and his parents before him. Who was Christopher Mellor now? Alex sat back in the chair and waited for the plane to start moving. It did, the captain taxied to the runway and took off. Back to Germany, Alex thought. As soon as they were up in the air she looked for food. The fridge had been restocked with an array of sandwiches and sushi for the flight and there were also some desserts. Alex took a sandwich and a bottle of water and went back to her seat. It was a quiet flight, the captain played classical music in the cockpit but very low, almost just to drown out the noise of the airplane.

Alex had arrived back in Germany and was fast tracked through customs again because of the private plane which gave her a status in public airports. The hire car was waiting on the other side. Whoever Mr Mellor was he was efficient. Alex had two choices, she knew Michael was going to go to the Institute but she also knew that Dr Smith was going to be a target at some point. She took the risk. She didn't give him Dr Smith's name and took the risk that Michael was going to need to find out more about the Institute before he went any further. She headed to the only hotel she knew close to the Institute. By chance the same place that Michael was staying.

Michael changed into the blue suit, with a white shirt and the brown shoes. He felt more like his old self than he had in days. He couldn't help thinking what a few days it had been. He wandered down to the lobby and ordered a drink at the bar, turning the heads of every young lady in the hotel and some of the men. Yes, this felt like being home. After a couple of drinks he headed out of the bar, through the lobby and into a cab. If he had turned back, or if the receptionist had not just approached Alex at that time they would have met there and then. But by the time Alex did turn around Michael's cab had just driven out of view. He headed for the bar called Passion. The taxi driver had told him it was a little early, but there were some nice bars in the area which he could drink in first. This was exactly what Michael wanted, a few drinks and a night out on the town.

Alex checked into her room and then was stumped what to do with the rest of the evening. Michael could have been anywhere and she was banking on him going to the Institute tomorrow. By now there would be no one left at the Institute and she didn't know where Dr Smith would be. The most she could do is sit downstairs, have a drink and plan out what she was going to do tomorrow.

Michael found a bar, not far from Passion, so it was in walking distance for his latest conquest. He had a feeling he was in the right neighbourhood. There were a lot of well dressed men around and very few women. He walked up to the bar and could feel all eyes upon him. Ordering a large whiskey he turned to lean backwards against the bar. Within minutes he had been approached by at least three guys all trying to strike up a conversation. Michael was indeed in his element.

Although it didn't feel the same as it once had. Back in his club, with the guys that he had picked up there, he had had a sense of shame about who he was and how he felt. Michael didn't feel like that any more, he was coming to grips with his murderous tendencies and his sexuality. He let guys buy him drinks and flirted with most of those who approached him. His head had started to swim with the attention.

A guy called Ivan had really taken his fancy, not as good looking as Chris whom he fully intended to meet later, but still built as if he could have been part of the German master race also. Ivan had bought Michael a few drinks and as he stood at the bar he could feel Ivan's hands continually touching his back. After a while Ivan whispered in his ear to go outside. It was a warm night and they made their excuses and walked outside the bar. Just to get some fresh air. Ivan pulled him down the alley and started to kiss him, strong passionate kisses. Michael responded, he felt comfortable for the first time with this, there was no rage, no disgust at himself, he just let it happen. Before he knew it Ivan was undoing his trousers and on his knees. Michael had his hands on the back of his head as Ivan went to work. Michael was in sheer disbelief that this was happening in an alleyway less than twenty-five feet from the bar they had just been drinking in. But it felt good, the rush, the excitement of getting caught, all of these were exhilarating. Michael's emotions were under control and so was he. Before, by now the rage would have taken over but not now. Michael could kill and keep it separate. Michael finished and Ivan did his trousers back up for him. They both went back and stood at the bar. Ivan had a reputation for this. Everyone in the bar was looking at Michael now as Ivan's latest conquest.

Michael finished his drink and when Ivan had gone to the toilet he disappeared over to Passion. Ivan was never aware of how lucky he had been that night to catch Michael off guard and in the process of a new beginning in his control.

Alex went down to the bar, the hotel had been quiet. There were a dozen business types all sitting by themselves around the room and Alex sat at the bar to have a drink. She ordered a large brandy and sat watching the football game on the TV behind the bar. She didn't really understand it, but it passed the time.

"Can I buy you a drink?"

Alex turned to see a well dressed man, quite handsome, standing next to her.

"No, its fine."

"Please, allow me, these places drive me insane. Everyone, at their own little tables, never talking to each other."

Alex turned and smiled, she had been thinking the same thing as she walked through the door.

"I promise I won't annoy you, should you want me to leave I will. See, I didn't even come over with one of my cheesy chat up lines."

"Yes, why didn't you do that? I may have let you buy me a drink."

"To be honest, I felt that given you are without doubt probably the most beautiful woman I have ever seen, you would have heard and rejected every line that I knew."

Alex laughed. She couldn't remember the last time that she had heard herself do that. "That was good."

"Not my best. John by the way."

"Well, John, give me your best and I will let you buy me a drink."

"That sounds like a deal but first, I have to ask, did it hurt?"

John had held his hand up to her face and looked directly into her eyes. Alex thought for a moment, she had been careful to conceal any bruises she had, she had been in a few too many scrapes lately but she was confident that there was nothing he could see.

"Did what hurt?" she asked, hoping he couldn't see anything.

"When you fell from heaven?" John smiled at her, and Alex smiled back.

"Alex, by the way, and I am drinking brandy."

John sat on the stool next to Alex.

"So, Alex, apart from being beautiful, what else do you do?"

"Oh you are full of them, aren't you?"

"It is a gift."

"I work for the Institute across the road. I am in Admin, not exciting really, just back to Head Office for a conference and a couple of days in Germany. And you, clearly when you are not an international playboy."

"It's true that is my part time job, but when I am not doing that I am a spy."

"A spy, eh?"

"Yes, covert operations mainly. I was just on the other side of the room wondering if I followed you home, would you keep me?"

Alex laughed again, that felt so good, the smile on her face felt warm and real, something she had been missing. John started to rub his eyes really hard.

"Are you okay?"

"Yes I am fine, I think there is something wrong with my eyes because I just can't take them off you." Just as he said that the barman walked over with both of their drinks. He placed them down and walked away to the sound of laughter.

John was a salesmen and he too had been there to visit the Institute. He sold them medical equipment for the legit part of the business. He was the welcome distraction that Alex needed after the last couple of days. The drinks continued to flow and the one liners kept coming. Alex hadn't laughed that hard since a BBQ at Paul's house over a year ago. It felt good to relax even if it was for a short while. For a moment she forgot all about the murders. Michael, Christopher, all of it disappeared into a one off night in Germany. But before they knew it, the barman was rounding up last orders. You could get a drink in the study after hours but they were out of time at the hotel bar.

"I guess that's it?"

"I guess it is."

"Okay, I will give you five seconds to give me your number or you can forget about going out with me forever."

Alex laughed again. "Okay, okay, I just need to find a pen."

Alex rolled up John's sleeve and wrote her number on his arm. She kissed him on the cheek and went over the lobby and into the elevator. John looked down at his arm. Alex's room 719.

Michael paid to get into Passion and went straight to the bar and ordered a drink. The club was starting to fill up. There was a ratio of one woman to every twenty men so Michael knew this wasn't a straight person's bar. It was actually the first gay club that he had been in. The openness of their sexuality was almost shocking to him. It wasn't like a straight club. Straight clubs like the one he owned were more reserved. Men pussyfooted around women and courted them to have the chance of maybe a kiss at the end of the night. Some people got lucky and maybe had an earlier kiss and left before the lights came on but not many. Here, at every turn men were kissing men, on the dance floor, at the bar. It was exhilarating, Michael's pulse was racing.

"I hoped you would wear the blue one."

Michael turned to see Chris standing behind him.

"Are you going to buy a fellow a drink?"

"Sure."

Michael turned to the bar and summoned over the barman. He ordered two of their most expensive whiskeys and handed one to Chris.

"I have never seen a black card before? I had heard about them but never seen one?"

Michael didn't say anything. Chris had already started to talk money. This could be exactly what he had hoped for now. He was more interested in the card than in him.

"They are rare."

"Who are you, Michael? That you can afford to be in that elite circle."

"I could tell you, but then I would have to kill you." Michael wasn't kidding, but he was going to tell him and then, then he knew he kept his promises.

Chris placed the drinks down and led them over to the dance floor. This was a new experience too for Michael to dance in a club surrounded by guys. He had danced but in straight clubs with women in the circle also. This was different; Chris's hands were everywhere and so were everyone else's in the nightclub. Michael was engulfed in a sea of men on the dance floor and he loved it.

It had got to one thirty a.m. and it was kicking out time for a week night. Chris hailed a cab and took them back to his apartment. It was a small place about five minutes from the town centre and the shop which he had met Michael in. They had spent most of the night making out on the dance floor and now it was time for the real deal.

As they entered the apartment Chris pulled Michael straight to the bedroom, undressed him piece by piece as if to preserve the clothes he had just sold him. Ten minutes later they stood naked facing each other. Chris grabbed Michael by the hair and forced him on the bed. He flipped Michael over onto his front and held him down with one hand. Michael didn't struggle. He lay there like a sleeping lion. Chris grabbed some KY jelly out of the drawer at the side of the bed and applied it to Michael's behind. Still playing the dominant, Michael was subservient. Michael had never gone this far with a man before. Ivan was a first for him in the alleyway earlier tonight and he was about to get his first real taste of being a gay man. Chris entered him hard. Michael felt it. It wasn't what he expected but it felt good, as Chris went harder and harder he pulled Michael's hair harder and harder, scratching his back. Michael started to wince in pain.

"Say my name!" Chris was taunting him. "Say my name!"

"Chris."

"Say my name, Michael, my name."

"Chris."

"That's right, I own you, Michael, you're mine." Chris entered Michael harder and harder. Michael's emotions were surfacing, he could feel himself getting lost in the moment.

"I own you. Spoilt little rich kid with lots of money, aren't you, Michael?"

Michael didn't say anything, he was rampant with desire, his heart was beating so fast.

"This is what we do to spoilt little rich kids, we show them, we show them who the boss is!"

Michael could feel Chris getting harder and harder inside him, he was close.

"Say my name! Say my name!"

"Christopher." Michael was shouting back.

"That's right, Michael, Christopher. Christopher is your daddy now."

They were the last words Christopher said. Michael had a realisation about exactly where he was. The words 'I am your daddy' and his father's name and the act they were currently engaged in took him over the edge. Michael pushed backwards and Christopher fell off the bed. Before he knew it Michael had pulled him by his hair back onto the bed and with one swift action broke his neck.

Christopher lay still on the bed. Michael had intended to kill him tonight, he knew what he wanted to do, but his new found desire and sexuality had been making him question how the night was going to pan out. His lust had got the better of him, but not in a way of suppression any more but in a way of enjoyment for the total act itself. Christopher had chosen his words poorly. The one thing that was going to rattle Michael at the moment was his father. And unknowingly Christopher stepped the boundaries.

Michael didn't bother to clean up or remove any of the evidence of what they had been up to. He simply got dressed and left the apartment. It was a short walk back to the hotel and he managed to charm another drink at the bar before going to bed, as there was nobody in the study. Tomorrow was an early day, he had a nine a.m. appointment at the Brown Institute and hopefully from there some answers.

Chapter 15

"Captain, something is not right." Chris had been trying Alex for over four days now.

"She left here on Monday morning and it is now Friday, no one has seen her."

The captain was tending to agree with him. Even after the shooting which took Paul's life she would show up almost every other day for the three months she was supposed to be on sabbatical. Just to sit in the office, just to be close to them. And when she wasn't there she was at her father and brother's precinct or at her parents' house when her father arrived home from work, just so that she could discuss cases, or police work.

"What have her parents said?"

"Nothing, they haven't heard from her either. And I have been past her apartment every day and she isn't there."

The captain didn't like it. Ignoring Chris Masters was one thing but not coming in or talking to her parents was another.

"I think we have messed up, Captain. Alex isn't Alex."

The captain wanted to answer that with 'obviously if she is sleeping with you now'.

"What about James?"

He could see James just walking into the open plan office behind him.

"James!" the captain bellowed and he entered the office.

"Close the door. Chris thinks there is something wrong with Alex, have you heard from her?"

"No."

"I am telling you, something is going on with her and my theory is something to do with that Institute and the Quaid case."

The captain looked directly at James. "I do agree with him. It's not like Alex not to have even tried to be here in the last week?"

James nodded. "I agree."

"I believe we have missed something, something that has Alex in turmoil. Her actions over the last three weeks aren't the Alex that we knew." Even Chris had to acknowledge that included sleeping with him.

"Is there anything that we can think of which may have got her back on that case?"

"No, we came back from Germany empty handed, there was nothing. Well nothing we could prove anyway." Alex had shared some of her thoughts and feelings with Chris the first night that they had slept together in Germany. But since then she never mentioned them again. The Mellors had been kind enough to support them on the trip with the planes, limos and hotels, but it didn't produce any results.

"Was there anywhere that Alex went alone during the last few days of the case? Anywhere she could have discovered anything that we don't know about?"

"Not really, Captain. Chris and I were with her most of the time."

"I know I am clutching at straws really to see what could have made her think differently."

"I know she didn't like the fact that the Mellor boy was still out there, I did catch her a couple of times looking him up on the internet."

171

"Okay, let's start there, the two of you go and see him. Softly, these people have powerful friends remember but let me know if he has seen Alex lately."

Alex woke in the hotel room alone. Jack had left in the early hours of the morning and gone back to his own room. Alex didn't want to make a thing of what happened last night. It was a one night affair. Something she had been doing often lately. She also didn't want Michael to see them together and people around her tended to end up dead. Her thought was that Michael would be around the Institute sometime today. So she was going to sit in the coffee shop across the road and watch the main gate to see if she could spot him. She dressed and headed downstairs in the lift.

As the doors opened in the lobby she could see him walking out of the front door. Her first thought was to run after him, but this was a busy reception area with loads of people checking out. She could hardly tackle him or shoot at him there. Besides, the plus point was she knew exactly where he was staying now. Here in the same hotel as she was.

Alex followed Michael, but with enough distance for him not to notice her. They were heading straight towards the Institute which is what she had predicted. He passed the coffee shop and crossed over the road. Alex stopped. She wasn't going to follow Michael into the Institute. She figured he would learn all he needed to in there in order for him to make his next move.

Michael was taken through security and to the reception area. At reception he gave his name and was asked to take a seat whilst one of the doctors would come and collect him for his nine a.m. appointment. It wasn't long before a Dr Davidson came to reception and collected Michael, taking him to an office on the third floor.

"Can I interest you in a coffee, Mr Mellor?"

"Yes. Thank you. White no sugar."

The doctor beckoned to his assistant who was working in the corner and she disappeared, and then brought back a tray.

"So you have some questions?"

"Yes, one or two."

"Do you want me to give you a brief background of what we do here and that might help?"

"Please do."

"Okay, the Brown Institute has now been operational for nearly forty years. Most of that was spent in Paris but we have recently moved to a bigger facility to accommodate the growth in our business. We are split into three factions, first and foremost we are a working hospital with over four hundred doctors and six hundred nurses. This is what we would consider our day job. Secondly we are a research centre so that we can strive to cure all matters of illness and thirdly, which I presume is where your questions are, we are a treatment facility that helps couples who struggle to conceive a baby naturally. We have helped couples give birth to hundreds of thousands of little children."

Michael's thoughts went directly to hundreds of thousands of murderers in the world. Dr Davidson had said this so proudly and with confidence. He clearly found what they had been doing acceptable.

"What made you choose Germany?"

"I didn't, actually I didn't want to move, but the powers that be and the investors thought a change of country would be best for the business."

"And the investors are?"

"A lot of them keep their identity secret so we don't really know."

173

Michael was quickly getting to the conclusion that this wasn't the guy that he needed to speak to. He wasn't high enough up the food chain to answer the questions he wanted answering. He was correct Dr Davidson didn't even know about the experiment; he was a consultant and a front facing customer services manager. He was there just to appease any guests coming through the door.

Michael pulled out his own file from the rucksack he was carrying. "I have a few questions about my file."

"Where did you get that?"

"It was a gift from my father, he sat me down and explained everything to me a couple of weeks ago, about me and my sister and I wanted to see for myself."

Dr Davidson was unnerved now. This guy had a copy of his own file which wasn't something he had seen before. He opened it and looked through. "It seems all in order."

"It does, does it? Other than the lettering on the front. Do you know what that is for?"

"I don't, sorry."

"Can I save us both some time, doctor? Can you go to your boss, the most senior man in this place and tell him Michael Mellor is in your office. Michael Mellor, the son of Christopher Mellor, the guy that built this facility and potentially has been funding the whole operation for the past thirty years is in your office and he has questions that will need to be answered before I leave here today."

Dr Davidson stood up almost immediately. Michael's tone wasn't from someone who was kidding and even on his pay check he had heard the name Christopher Mellor. He made his excuses and left.

Chris and James arrived at the Mellor mansion. Christopher had agreed to a noon meeting at the house. They were showed into the study and stood awaiting his arrival.

"Morning, detectives, take a seat, and how may I be of assistance?"

"Thank you for your time, Mr Mellor. We were just revisiting the last case we spoke about and were wondering if you had heard anymore from the Brown Institute?" Chris didn't want to start the conversation with 'I think we have lost one of our detectives, can you tell me where your murderous son is?'.

"I am sorry to have wasted your time, detectives. The last time I heard anything about that was the day that you and, I want to say Detective Keaton, were leaving the house."

"Yes, Detective Keaton."

Christopher wasn't a stupid man. He knew they weren't there for this. This was something to do with Alex, either she was missing or they were worried.

"How is Miss Keaton?"

"She is fine, taking a couple of weeks holiday."

They don't know where she is, Christopher thought, that is why they are really here.

"Must be the season for it."

"Sorry?"

"Michael and Maria have been in Italy for a few days, she has just returned but Michael is staying a little longer, I presume."

"That's nice, when did they go?"

"Just Sunday, Maria came back yesterday."

Chris didn't know whether to be worried or not. Michael left the country on Sunday and Alex hadn't been seen from Monday. It was either a trick or he had done something or the Mellors weren't going to be of any use. There was a tension in the air as to who was going to ask the next question. Finally it was James that did.

"Mr Mellor, can I ask you a question about Detective Keaton?"

"Yes sure, but I am not sure I will be able to help you."

"When she came back from Germany did she seem okay to you?" It was at this point Chris looked directly at him. That was almost a question to him to say, did something go on that neither of you are telling us about.

"She seemed fine, a little upset as I don't believe she found what she was looking for, but fine I think. I believe her words to me were she needed to wrap this up and move on. The Quaid case I believe? Wouldn't you agree, Dr Masters?"

Chris was still looking at James to see why he would ask that question. "Yes, I agree."

"In fact, I think she said something about visiting Jack's father and wife Dee, was it? And then getting back to normal."

Christopher had used the opportunity to start the process of Alex's demise. The detectives in front of him weren't looking for thousands of murderers, they were looking for their partner. Which had told him that they didn't know why she would have been hunting down Michael. Once Alex had done the dirty work for him, he was going to have to take care of her. What better than to put the police on her trail.

"Well, if there is nothing else, detectives?"

"Sorry, no, we have taken up enough of your time."

Chris and James made their exit and headed back to the car.

"What was that about?"

"I was just asking if we have missed something. If Alex had found something we didn't know about."

Chris didn't know what to make of James. He had always been the silent type with no ambition to be anything else. It wasn't like him to ask questions, especially good questions.

"All I am saying is that Alex is a good detective, probably one of the best we have. If anyone was going to find something, she would have."

Chris knew this to be true also. He had been working over in his head for the past week to see if he had missed something. She wasn't alone all the time they were in Germany, other than the tests they had done on them. She didn't mention knowing something, but then he was never one hundred per cent sure that she trusted him.

"I think the father or Dee is worth a visit, don't you?"

"Yes, let's start with his dad; I think that's who Jack Quaid would have confided in, before his estranged wife, if we have missed something."

Michael had been waiting for almost thirty minutes. Before Chris and James had arrived at the mansion, Christopher Mellor had received a call from Dr Smith telling him his son was there and asking questions. Christopher played his part well stating that his son had just found out and that he told him if he had questions that would be the best place to start. Dr Smith entered the office without Dr Davidson.

"Mr Mellor? I am Doctor Jonathan Smith."

"Hi, you must be the boss?"

"That I am, Mr Mellor. So you have some questions, which is totally understandable. I am sure it came as quite a shock when your father told you last week."

Michael wasn't sure but the way he said that implied that he had spoken to his father. He wasn't about to say 'Michael found out from a detective whom I have hired to kill him'.

"Yes it did, we were told a totally different story originally."

"That is not uncommon, Mr Mellor. The process we used back then was not as commonplace as today. So fire away."

"My first question is, what do the letters mean on the front of the file?"

Dr Smith was stopped in his tracks, the second time in as many months he had been asked this question. "Which letters would these be?"

"These." Michael handed the files to Dr Smith. This time it wasn't just the letters but Michael had a copy of the file. They have never released these files.

"Can I ask…" Before he could finish the sentence Michael butted in.

"My father." Dr Smith knew this was a lie, well, at least he hoped it was a lie. Not even he would have been given a copy. Unless he was the one who created the break-in in Paris. Dr Smith was off his game. He had the feeling he was being set up here somehow.

"It is simple really. It is just the initials of the doctors who were looking after your parents' cases. Martin and Peterson if I recall."

Michael knew it was a lie, it was written all across his face. All those years of people watching with Maria had paid off.

"Oh okay. Can I meet them?"

Dr Smith was stumped at the question. "Sorry?"

"Can I meet the doctors who brought me to life?"

"I am sorry, Mr Mellor, but neither of those gentlemen are with us any more."

Another lie. Michael knew this man had all the answers but wasn't going to share any of them. Dr Smith knew from the file who and what he was so he needed to be careful with what he said.

"No problem, it was worth a shot." Michael had him on the ropes but he needed him on his side. This guy was going to give him answers but not here.

"So I understand that my father is an investor? Is there a return on his investment? Is it something I should be looking at also? I mean given that this facility has given me so much?"

This had Dr Smith back into work mode, he knew that Michael had money given by his father and he was always keen to collect more of that.

"It is a modest return, Mr Mellor, and I believe it helps with the taxman given that we are also a charity."

"That is always good news, is there any chance of a tour?"

"Definitely, Mr Mellor, I will escort you myself."

Dr Smith got up and walked Michael to the door. "Maybe a spot of lunch afterwards, if it suits, Mr Mellor?"

"Sounds good."

Alex was still sat in the coffee shop across the road. There was little she could do other than wait for Michael to reappear. She did think of warning Dr Smith that he was a potential target, but also thought that maybe he had this coming to him. He knew what he was creating, did he really think at one point he wasn't going to have to answer for this?

Chris and James arrived at Jack's dad's place. He welcomed them in.

"Can I get you a coffee, gents?"

"Only if you are having one."

"I have a pot on the go already." Jack's dad brought in a tray. Coffee, milk and a few biscuits on the side. He hadn't had many visitors lately. In fact, since Alex, the only person that had come to see him was Dee. "How can I help you?"

"We are just following up on your son's case and wondered if you had remembered anything else that you would have liked to tell us?"

"I am confused, gents. I thought it was ruled as a suicide."

"It was, but with suicides we also want to do a follow up call, just to see if potentially we could have missed something."

"Well, I think we had covered everything. My son was a troubled man, Detective, I know his heart was in the right place and he always tried to do everything he could for everyone else. But he was troubled nonetheless."

Jack's father had poured the coffee and all three were sitting back now drinking it.

"How is the young detective, the pretty woman? I can't seem to remember her name."

"Missing," James piped up. Chris hadn't expected those words.

"Missing?"

"Yes missing, sir. She hasn't been seen for a few days. She may have taken a holiday but it would not be like her if she did."

"That's worrying. Is that why you are really here?"

"Yes, sir." James was fed up of lying and pussy footing around. This wasn't going to help them find Alex. The meeting at the Mellor's house had got him riled.

"You don't think I have anything to do with it?"

"Of course not, sir." Chris thought he had better take over the conversation. Jack's dad was an old man and he didn't need to be thinking the police had him in questioning.

"We were just wondering if you had seen Miss Keaton lately or there was anything that you spoke to her about that we should have known about."

"I don't think so. She was always ever so busy and about to run off somewhere. If I recall, my memory isn't what it used to be I am afraid."

"When was the last time you saw her?"

"It was the day she came back from Germany, that morning actually." This tied up with what Mr Mellor had said. She wanted to close the case down and move on.

"And what did you discuss?"

"Just that she had been returning from Germany, the fact that you had been investigating the Brown Institute. As had my son but came home empty handed."

Chris and James looked at each other, why would she tell him all this? She had told him the whole story.

"Why do you think your son was investigating the Brown Institute, sir?"

"I didn't know he was at first, I wish I had, I could have saved him some time. You see, Detective, we travelled a lot when I was younger and we were struggling to have a baby. My wife, she was already going googly eyes at every passing pram and we needed help. That's why we signed up. If I had known Jack had been there I would have sat him down and explained everything to him."

"Signed up to what?"

"The Brown Institute. Sorry I would have expected the young lady to have told you."

She hadn't told them, she hadn't told them that Jack was a product of the facility. How was this going to play out? Neither Chris nor James believed in coincidences.

"No sorry, she didn't."

"Oh, I presumed it was all going to be in the letter."

"The letter?"

"Yes, the letter, Detective, the one Jack left with me, which I handed to her the day she came back from Germany."

Alex hadn't mentioned to either of them about a letter.

"What was in the letter, Mr Quaid?"

"I don't know, I didn't want to read it. I presumed that you had? I believe it was some kind of theory or evidence to prove whatever Jack had been up to. I thought at first he was just looking into where he was born. But he was too emotional for that. He had something on his mind."

They were right, Alex knew more than she had been letting on. They both knew Alex was a private person; she didn't share her theories very often and not openly to all. But this time she had purposely kept information from them. She had kept this from all of them.

"And do you know what theories your son had?"

"No, Detective, I was still ashamed of not telling him about the Brown Institute earlier. I was hoping that where he was born wasn't going to get found out. But I knew Jack and I also knew he wouldn't give up. When he came here with the letter, I tried to persuade him to drop it but he didn't. He knew that something would happen when he got to Germany or around Germany but I didn't think it would end with him taking his own life." Jack's dad had started to well up with the thought of Jack's suicide.

"If he had just come to me, on his return. I could have explained why we did what we did."

Chris and James knew there was little else they were going to get from him. He had had the evidence but Alex had it now and she was missing.

"I think we should go, sir, thank you for the coffee and your time."

"Oh okay, I am sorry I couldn't have been any more help, Detective, but I would advise a visit to Dee. I am sure if you want to know more then she will be able to help you. And I hope your friend turns up."

Chapter 16

"It's a silver service restaurant, Mr Mellor, so let's get a table over by the window and the waitress will come and take our order."

Dr Smith had given Michael the full tour of the facility, introducing him to members of staff as he went. Michael couldn't help thinking: 'Are you the guy, are you the guy who put that gene into me?' Every one of them deserved what was coming to them. But most of all Dr Smith deserved what was coming to him. He knew so much more than he was sharing.

"May I join you?" Dr Smith's daughter, Alana, had come to the table. All of the hospital was abuzz over the guy who was walking around with Dr Smith. Stunningly handsome with the most amazing eyes. Alana had to see for herself.

"Mr Mellor, this is my daughter, Alana." Michael got up and pulled out the chair for her.

"It's Michael, Mr Mellor is my father." Michael had very little interest in women, but he did know how to use them to get what he wanted.

"Hi, Michael, what brings you here?"

"My father is an investor and I was looking to see if I should be also. I must say I am very impressed with what I have seen so far, especially now." Michael whispered that as if directly to Alana. Her father had been talking to the waitress to ensure they had the correct wine with the meal.

"Are you American, Mr, sorry, Michael?"

"European actually but spent a lot of my time in the USA. So did your father make you move here as well when they relocated the business?"

"Alana works here too, Mr Mellor. She is our Senior Admin Manager and hopefully soon Director of Admin." Michael thought she must know the code then if she is in charge of admin.

"My dad speaks out of turn. I have only applied for the role, there is no proof that I will get it."

"But being the boss's daughter always helps." Alana smiled at Michael. The girls from admin hadn't lied to her. She had been fixated by his eyes from the moment they sat down.

"Alana does everything on her own, Mr Mellor. She is a very independent person."

"I am sure she does, Dr Smith, I was just teasing."

"So how is your father, Christopher?"

Michael's mind went back to last night. My father. My daddy, Christopher. There was still a dead body with his DNA all over it about a ten minute walk from where they were, just because he brought up Michael's daddy issues.

"Mr Mellor?"

"Yes, sorry, yes, he is good. Recently been to Italy with my sister and I believe back home now." Michael wanted to change the subject off his father as soon as possible.

"So, Alana, do you miss Paris? How is living in Germany?"

"It's fine. I haven't found a place yet so still living with my parents until I do. But I am enjoying the nightlife in Germany."

"There is a night life? I hadn't noticed. I arrived yesterday and found it a very sleepy town."

Michael was in full on flirt mode with Alana. She had said the magic words that she still lived with her father. If he could get the address from her, he would get the answers to the questions he had.

Lunch continued and they discussed investment in the facility. Alana and Michael discussed the area, best places to go, best places to eat. Michael had said he was going to stay on for a couple of days and make a nice break out of it, given that this was his first visit. As lunch was coming to a close Dr Smith made his excuses and let Alana show Michael out of the building.

"Well, it was a pleasure, Miss Smith."

"It was indeed, Mr Mellor." Alana was laughing back at him. She took a business card out of her pocket and handed it to him. She hadn't been this forward since she met Jack about a month ago. Although that didn't end well with him disappearing, Alana was convinced this was a guy she wanted to know. "My direct number is on there and my mobile, should you want to get a coffee or go for a drink."

"Thank you, I will definitely be doing that."

Michael left the building.

Alex was tracking Michael from the moment he left. He turned right out of the facility and headed towards the town. Alex finished her drink and stayed behind him as he walked to the centre. There didn't seem to be a destination to his walk until he passed a hardware shop and went inside. She could see him through the window collecting merchandise. Rope, tape, and a hammer. Michael was stocking supplies. She had seen firsthand what he could do with a hammer and he had been intending to do it again. She followed him as he came out of the shop and then he headed back to the hotel. On entering reception he went to the counter and picked up his key. He was on the floor below Alex and he headed up in the elevator.

What now, thought Alex, what was her next move? She knew Michael had answers or else he would not have been stocking up on goods. But what did that mean to her? What was she going to do about it? She could barge the room like he had done in Rome and make a scene but that wasn't going to stop Michael. She could try and reason with him. But she didn't see that working either. The only thing she could think of was to wait and see if she could catch him in the act. If she could she could end this and still have a somewhat credible reason for what she was doing.

Alex returned to the bar where she had been the night before and situated herself within view of all elevators. She ordered the club sandwich and an orange juice and set herself in for the afternoon. She would wait for Michael until he made his move.

Chris and James drove to Dee's house but there had been no one home. They left a note through the door for her to call them immediately on her return. They decided to drive to Alex's father's precinct. Maybe he had known more than he was letting on. On arrival they were ushered through to him and Jason.

"Have you heard from her?"

"No, I haven't and I am getting really worried now. How about either of you? Has Alex phoned home?"

"No, straight through to answerphone most of the time and her mother is starting to worry." Alex's father had been trying to reassure her but it wasn't doing any good.

"Do you think it has anything to do with the Deacon James' case?"

"No I don't, this is something to do with the Quaid suicide."

"Are you sure? This whole Deacon James thing is unravelling on the news. They are saying he could have killed hundreds and he had followers, maybe one of those has got to Alex." Jason wasn't thinking like a brother, he was thinking like a cop. He got the look from his father, though, who was thinking like a concerned parent.

"I think she found out something about the Brown Institute."

"The place you visited in Germany?"

"Yes, I can't be sure yet, but I think Alex was onto something and she hasn't been sharing it with us. Something to do with the Institute and what goes on there."

"Like what?"

"I don't know."

"What I do know is this, I have run her passport and she has been to Italy."

"Italy?" Chris now had butterflies in his stomach. "Italy? When did she go to Italy?"

"Monday, apparently. I have no records of her returning but she was on a first class flight out of here Monday morning."

"But she was in the office Monday morning? The captain gave her two weeks off due to the Deacon James' debacle."

"Well, she must have left directly after that."

"Then I think she is in trouble as Michael Mellor is in Italy and that can't be a coincidence."

"Wasn't he the guy that stabbed the young man in the nightclub?"

"Yes, but Alex let him off with it in order to get to the Brown Institute. She didn't like that fact and she told me, she told all of us that she wasn't going to let him get away with it." Chris was positive of this.

Alex was going to get Michael one way or another and now they were both out of the country.

"So how do we get to her?"

"I don't know, James; we don't want to get the police involved."

"I would suggest we go back to the Mellor's residence and have a conversation with his father. If Michael has been in contact with Alex then he will surely know."

Chris beckoned to James to get moving.

"Keep in touch, Jason, and I will keep trying to get a hold of her and start to look for hotels booked in her name. Let's see if we can find where she is staying."

"Will do and I will call you after the Mellors."

Alex had been downstairs waiting for Michael all afternoon. She didn't even leave to go to the bathroom and after five coffees and a few orange juices this was getting uncomfortable. About six p.m. Michael appeared from the lift dressed in his blue suit that he had worn last night, with a white open top shirt. He spoke to reception and within five minutes a limo had picked him up outside. He was carrying his rucksack which he placed in the boot of the limo. This was it. Michael was about to make his move. As the limo took off Alex called the next cab in line and paid the driver an additional twenty euros to follow the limo. He didn't ask questions which was good as Alex didn't have the answers.

The limo drove towards the Institute. On arrival there was a young woman waiting outside for him. She entered the car and it drove off. Alex followed in a cab until she got to a restaurant. Michael walked around, opened the door for the lady and went inside. This woman had to be important. Michael was show boating and to a woman, which certainly wasn't his style.

"You didn't have to order a limo."

"Like I said, I am grateful you are showing me around."

The waiter took them over to the table and they sat down.

"So, you recommended the place. What is good here?"

"To be honest, I have no idea. I just know people talk about it all the time. I wasn't exactly thinking you were going to book it."

"Then we will learn together."

Chris and James were back in the study awaiting Christopher Mellor.

"Gentlemen, twice in one day?"

"Yes we are sorry, sir, but we have learnt something that may be concerning to you."

"Which is?"

"Which is, that Alex Keaton is missing and we now believe she is in Rome, and it is also concerning that your son is there also."

"So Miss Keaton has gone to Rome to see my son? That is worrying. Why would she be doing that?"

"We don't know."

"Well she swore, didn't she, that Michael had nothing to do with that stabbing in the club, so why would she be following my son?"

"Again, sir, we don't know. You said your daughter had returned recently, can she shed any light on this?"

Christopher nodded to one of the guards in the corner who left the room and within a couple of minutes returned with Maria.

"Come and sit over here, dear, these gentlemen have just informed me that the detective from the club is missing and presumed in Rome with Michael."

"With our Michael?"

"Well, at least close to Michael. Did you see her whilst you were there?"

"No, it was just Michael, me and Harry." Maria's voice broke at the point. She hadn't supposed to say Harry, it just came out. Harry was now at the bottom of the river. She didn't want to think about that.

"We had a couple of days shopping, went to the charity event at the Vatican and then visited a few sites. Michael didn't want to come home yet as the weather was good and he was enjoying the city. Said he would be home in the next couple of days."

"Were you with your brother all the time, Miss Mellor?" Maria knew what that implied and she was hardly going to say 'other than the time he drugged me'.

"Yes, Detective, as I said a little shopping and some sightseeing. We both love Rome as a city."

"I must say, Detective, I am not happy about the police following my son halfway across the world when he hasn't done anything. I will be speaking to the commissioner if this is true."

Neither Chris nor James had an answer for him. They couldn't explain why Alex would have jumped on a plane to go and see Michael any more than Christopher could.

"I understand, sir, but until we have all the facts I am not going to comment."

"Well, Detective, I suggest you go and find some."

"If you could let us know if your brother sees Detective Keaton that would be a great help."

Maria nodded back in his direction but didn't say anything. James and Chris had left empty handed and probably started a shit storm for the captain. But they needed to do something in order to find Alex and quick. The recap they did in the car included Alex withholding information and hunting down a suspect in an attempted murder whom she had personally acquitted and stood up for even though she knew he did it. All ways up from this didn't look good on her.

Chapter 17

Alex managed to find a coffee shop that was opposite the restaurant, realising there was now one on every corner in every city. She managed to take her eyes off of them long enough to go to the toilet. They weren't going anywhere, he was on a date with the young girl and he wasn't about to rush out. She watched them through mains and dessert. He had halved his dessert and gave it to her. He really wanted her to know he was interested. Michael on the other hand was playing the great listener, learning all about the Institute, her father, everything he could glean from her. It was a lot and Alana was an open book. They talked about their new house, the layout, the security systems. Alana had just been too trusting, as she had with Jack and the password to her computer. She even told Michael the number to disarm the silent alarm in the house, and how it had been her birthday. Her dad loved her that much. Michael finished up dinner with Alana and as Alex could see them grabbing their coats she could see the limo arriving outside. It was time, they were on the move again.

There was still no word on Dee. Chris and James headed back to the station to fill in the captain.

"Italy?"

"So her father reckons, Alex's passport was triggered on Monday after she left here."

"And you think she has gone after Michael Mellor?"

"That was our initial thought, wasn't it, James?" James nodded in the corner.

"But you don't believe that now?"

"I think there is more to it, Captain. I think she knows more than she has been letting on. We have been to see Mr Quaid's father. He told us he gave Alex a letter, a letter from her son, that he believed either had evidence or a theory about the Brown Institute and she never mentioned it to us."

"So?"

"So, I don't know what, but there are too many holes in what has been going on. There is some proof of wrongdoings in the Institute. We went there, we couldn't find anything. Alex has something and now she is hunting down one of the children that was born there. It stinks to me, Captain, something isn't quite right."

"So what do we do next?"

"Alex's father and brother are going to continue the search for her in Italy. We have been to the Mellors and warned them that she is in Italy and should Michael spot her we need to know."

"She isn't the criminal here, Chris." The captain was starting to feel like they were on a witch hunt for Alex.

"No, I know she isn't but I am not sure she is in her right mind. Whatever has been going on with Alex in the last month, I do agree with you, Captain. It's out of character for her."

The captain had been saying this for weeks; she was indeed all over the place of late, including her choice in men.

"And what can we do? Just sit here and wait?"

"No, not sit and wait, we have to dig more into the Institute I feel, whatever this is. That is in the centre of it all."

"James and I are waiting for a call back from Dee, Mr Quaid's estranged wife. I also think that if anyone has any more information on this it is going to be her."

"Okay, doesn't sound like we have a lot to go on."

"We don't, but if we are to find out what Alex is up to and get her back we need to act fast. She was convinced that Michael Mellor was a murderer and so am I. She is not safe where she is."

Michael had been the perfect gentleman on the date – attentive, funny, handsome and clever. It wasn't until he got in the back of the limo with Alana he felt uncomfortable. She had kissed him. Not softly but full on. He needed to respond but kissing a girl wasn't something he had a lot of experience in. He closed his eyes and thought of the night before, not Christopher as he needed to remain in control. But Ivan and the bar full of men. They had all been like bees to nectar as he stood at the bar. His mind wandered as they continued to kiss.

"You need to tell the driver where to drop you off," Michael whispered in her ear.

"I can come back to your hotel if you like?" Michael knew that wasn't the plan.

"Never on a first date, Miss Smith. You are the only reason I stayed in Germany today. I would have flown back if it wasn't for our lunch. I would really like to get to know you some more."

Alana was taken back and so glad to hear those words. Somebody who wanted to stick around for her was exactly what she needed. Jack standing her up had been one of a series of relationships ending that way. She was starting to believe that it was her. She was having this effect on men.

"Okay, that sounds perfect." Alana told the driver the address of the house. Michael's plan had worked. He was about to go to Dr Smith's house. He didn't know that Alex was following close behind.

On arrival at the house Alex watched as the limo drove up the driveway. It was set off the road by about a quarter of a mile. Ten minutes later the young woman exited the vehicle and stood in the doorway. The limo proceeded to drive away and she entered. As the car turned out of the driveway it parked about a hundred yards down the street. Michael got out and opened the boot of the car and retrieved his rucksack. Alex paid the cab and waited for him to disappear up the drive before it took off, leaving Alex in the shadows.

Chris was sitting in Alex's chair in the office with James at his own desk. "So what shall we do while we wait for Dee to call?"

"I don't know. I am feeling a little useless at the moment."

"I know what you mean."

"I will say something though, I know it will sound odd but that Oliver Gordon case we had, I will swear Alex knew he had done it before she walked in their apartment."

"Really, how come?"

"Yeah, I don't know why but I just had this feeling that she had already made up her mind who had done this, and then she was just going to get him. It was almost as if she was just baiting him to confess."

"But isn't that what you all do as detectives? A little cat and mouse?"

"Yeah, but not like this. And then there is the Deacon James thing. That doesn't make any sense either."

"What makes you say that?"

"When have you ever known Alex to drive anywhere? She hates driving. I can't see her deciding to jump in a car and take a three hour drive in the direction of nothing. She doesn't have family or friends that way. Even if you just wanted a drive, an hour maybe two in one direction but not three and a half as that almost feels like you were planning an overnight."

James was right, Alex had been planning an overnight. It had been a two day BBQ fun day and she wasn't convinced it was all going to happen on the first night.

Chris's phone rang with an unknown number. "Alex?"

"No, er sorry, you left your card in my door. It is Dee, Dee Quaid."

"Ah yes, Mrs Quaid. Look I know it is getting late but my partner and I just need a couple of questions answering. We could be with you in less than thirty minutes. I wouldn't normally ask but time is of the essence."

"Sure, I am home all evening now, Detective, just finished my art class."

Chris hung up the phone. "Come on, Dee is home."

James grabbed their coats and they headed for the door.

Alex was careful to keep Michael in her eye line at all times. She didn't want to be surprised by him. He walked up the driveway in darkness and she followed. When he got within viewing distance of the house he stopped. He opened his bag and took out what looked to be a gun. Her gun, the one he had taken from the cabin. He then proceeded to walk the perimeter of the residence. There were several lights on in the house but she couldn't see anyone inside. When they got around to the back of the house she could see Dr Smith in his study talking with the young lady. It must have been his daughter, that's why Michael was on the charm offensive. She had led him straight back to her father. Dr Smith kissed the young girl on the forehead and she disappeared out of sight, a couple of minutes later a light went on in one of the rooms upstairs. Alex thought she must have gone to bed.

Michael was still sitting in the bushes. He wasn't making a move. What was he waiting for? Alex was thankful it was a warm night as they sat there for a further twenty minutes, neither of them moving until Dr Smith turned off the light and disappeared. More lights were being turned off as he walked through the house towards his bedroom. Then another light appeared on upstairs, that was Michael's move. Michael had done a good job with Alana. He had made her give up the layout of the house, the silent alarm and a way into the house which was normally open. There was a side door which she used when she was late home. She always left it open on the off chance of a later night out and not wanting to wake her parents. There was no alarm here, but she hadn't told them, and if you were quick enough you could get over to the kitchen and switch off all of the alarms around the house before anyone knew you were there. Alana had practically given Michael the front door keys and said come in.

Michael followed her instructions to the letter and before he knew it he was standing in Dr Smith's kitchen. Alex had managed to get to the door and could see him tampering with the alarm system.

Chris and James arrived at Dee's house. She was painting in the kitchen, finishing the work from her art class.

"Come in, sorry about the mess. I am finishing up my latest project."

"Not a problem, Mrs Quaid, sorry to call at such a late hour."

"I don't think I am Mrs Quaid any more, with Jack gone I am not sure I am a Mrs anything any more."

"Sorry, I didn't mean to upset you."

"No need to apologise, I am just trying to get used to it. I find myself thinking about using my maiden name but can't quite bring myself to making the change. Silly really."

"Anyway we don't want to take up much of your time."

"Take as long as you like, would you like a coffee?"

"Only if you are having one also." Chris never refused coffee. It is what kept him going most days.

"Yes, I was about to." Dee stood over in the kitchen area and proceeded to make coffee for all three of them. "So you said it was urgent?"

"Kind of, I will be straight with you, Mrs Qu..., Dee. Sorry. Have you seen Detective Keaton lately?"

"No, I don't believe so."

"When was the last time you saw her?"

"I think she had just come back from Germany, from the Brown Institute I think."

Chris and James were surprised again. Had Alex shared everything with these people? Everyone knew about Germany, the Brown Institute. Between Jack's father and Dee they knew more about the case than they did.

"And was she okay? Did she seem okay to you?"

"Yes I think so, sugar either of you?"

"No thanks, the caffeine is enough normally." James nodded his head also.

"Why do you ask?"

"She is missing." James couldn't hold in that part of the information any more.

"Missing?" Dee turned around with a concerned look on her face. "What do you mean missing?"

"Well, she was given leave on Monday and nobody has seen her since." James was getting more and more upset at the notion that she was gone.

"We believe she has gone to Italy, do you know of any reason she would do that Dee? I hate to ask but we are retracing her steps over the last month to see if we have missed anything."

Dee took the coffee into the living area and placed it on the table. She gestured for them both to sit down, which they did. "I am sorry no; I don't know anything about Italy other than they have some fantastic art there. And I certainly don't know anyone in Italy either."

"Okay, thanks, it was a long shot, but after we spoke to Jack's dad he thought if anyone had any more information it would be you."

"Oh, you spoke with him did you? How is he? I have been meaning to get to him for weeks now but never really find the time."

"He seems fine. Dee, is there anything else that you think could be useful around your husband's case or about Alex that we haven't already explored?"

Dee sat back and thought, there was nothing, she had shared everything she knew with Alex.

"There really isn't, I mean I only met the woman a couple of times and I think on most of those times I wasn't myself. I was still grieving the loss of my husband. Obviously it got a lot easier, sorry faster, but that's done now."

Chris listened to those words again in his head. It got faster, easier to grieve for her husband, is that what she just said?

"A drop more coffee?"

"No, thank you. I am sorry to pry, Dee, but did you just say it got easier to grieve, no faster to grieve for your husband?"

"Yes, when I found out, at first I was mad, mad that I hadn't seen it. Mad that someone could have done that, but then I started to think about it and it wasn't really his fault. I guess it is why I don't want to face his father too, as I know it is not his fault either it is just what happened."

Chris was still trying to take in what she was saying. It was as if he was watching Jack's video again in the captain's office, she was talking in riddles.

"Dee, can you slow down a bit."

"Sorry, what have I said?"

"Are you talking about Jack and the Brown Institute?"

"Yes, I thought you knew about that?"

"Yes, we do, Dee, but we only found out a short while ago, and you are upset with him, or were upset with him for being born there, and his father for not telling him?"

"No, I understand any parent wants to tell their child that they weren't naturally born, not naturally, you know what I mean; boy girl, not boy girl dish doctor. I do understand why it didn't come up in conversation over dinner."

"Sorry, again, what is it you are actually saying?"

"I am saying that I forgave him quicker and moved on quicker once I understood what they had done to him. Sorry, what they had done to them. You know, the children."

Chris was looking at James, she knew the answer. Dee knew the answer.

"What they had done to him?"

"Yes, about his obsessions, and his obsessive nature, Detective. Like the rest of them. He was always that way but I just put it down to being Jack. All those years in the coffee shop. The time he spent there every day just to see me. I didn't know that they had made experiments of them all, I didn't know that it wasn't just Jack, he wasn't the only one and it clearly wasn't just obsessions. When I found out about the murderers and the psychopaths I was just thankful that is all that they gave him."

Chris's head had started to swim, he was looking at James but he convinced himself pretty quickly James had lost the train of the conversation.

"The Brown Institute has been doing experiments on children with regards to what, traits, genes, behaviour patterns and Jack was one of them?"

It was Dee's turn to look surprised at the questioning. "Yes, that is what I have been saying. Surely you know this, Detective. I gave Alex the hard drive with it all on, there must have been a hundred thousand murderers on there."

Chapter 18

Alex followed Michael into the kitchen as he headed out of it into the hallway. She knew it was dangerous, but if she was going to catch him she wanted to catch him in the act. It was some kind of justification for what she was about to do. There was a timing issue though; she knew what he had done at Paul's parents' house, fast and rash. Then there was what he had done to Mike. Basically killed him in his sleep, without making a sound. She figured that he would probably want answers from Dr Smith though so it wasn't going to be a fast process.

She watched him disappear out of sight on the stairs before following up.

Michael went through the door of Dr Smith's bedroom. He was a sound sleeper and lay quite still on the bed. His wife was at a charity event and wasn't returning this evening so that had been a blessing. Alana had told Michael over dinner so he started to put his plan into action. As he walked over to the bed, Dr Smith stirred. Michael grabbed him and forced his hand over his mouth. Dr Smith struggled but Michael was clearly the stronger person.

Michael whispered to him. "You know what I am?"

Dr Smith nodded.

"And you know what I am capable of?"

He nodded again.

"Your daughter is two rooms down and still asleep. I am going to take my hand off of your mouth, you are going to put your gown on and walk downstairs with me quietly. We are going to have a little chat about what has been going on. Okay?"

Dr Smith nodded for the third time.

"The alarms are disabled and if you make a sound or scream for help I will kill both of you here tonight."

Michael let go of his mouth, Dr Smith did as he was told and got dressed. Given everything that he had been working on over the last forty years he wasn't surprised about what was happening. He often dreamt that this was going to happen one day.

Alex watched them both as they left the room. Michael was standing behind the doctor with a gun to the back of his head. She was hiding around the corridor. It was complete silence. If she had still been a policewoman she would have run into Alana's room as they went downstairs, told her to call the police and then waited for backup. But tonight she wasn't a policewoman. Tonight she was working for Christopher Mellor and avenging the deaths of Paul's family. Tonight she was one of the hundred thousand.

"What hard drive? What are you on about?"

"The hard drive I gave Detective Keaton. Surely she told you about it?"

Chris and James were just staring directly at each other.

"Dee, I think you are going to have to explain a bit more, from the beginning, slowly so we can take it all in."

"Okay, when Jack shot himself I was so upset. I couldn't help but think it was all my fault for leaving him. I went to see Alex at the house and she was, well I am not really sure what she was doing. But she said I could go back into the house in a couple of days to start to clear Jack's

204

stuff up. I waited and then I got a call from a young lady at your station who said I could go back in. It was nice that your men had cleared up most of the blood and taken the sheets away. But I started to go through Jack's things, just spring cleaning really and boxing some of his clothes up for a charity. It was either that or give them to his father. I am not sure he would have wanted them though."

Chris was starting to wish he hadn't said from the beginning, he was only interested in the facts.

"Anyway this hard drive was in his jacket pocket. Quite shocking really, as I would have put money on Jack not knowing what a hard drive was. I put it to one side but it kept playing on my mind. Jack had only had a computer or laptop thingy for about a year, and to be honest he only ever wrote his journal on it I think. So I took it home and opened it."

"And what was on it?" James had been practically invisible up until this point but could feel this was the answer they had been looking for.

"At first I thought it was just a list of some kind, there were names, dates of birth and last known addresses and a column which just had lettering in it. Only five or six letters in each but some similar, some not so similar. I almost ignored it at first and then I remembered what I had read one day, back when I was living with Jack. It was in one of his books, he had asked me whether I thought people were tampered with. I decided to look at it a little more closely. There were a couple of search fields where I could look for names, dates of birth and the letter coding. I am ashamed to say it but I put Jack's name in first and it came up, OC. I didn't need to be a detective to work that one out. Obsessive compulsive disorder. I then tried another, a case Jack had been obsessed with, Stephen McAndrew, and as large as life there he was, MPOC. Given I knew the case from the papers I worked the coding out also. Murderous, psychopath, obsessive, compulsive. From there it wasn't a great stretch to see what the list was. It was a download from the Brown Institute with all the names of the children that have been through there."

There was silence; neither James nor Chris could believe what they had just heard.

"Sit down." Michael pointed over to the desk and Dr Smith sat down. Michael was pacing up and down.

"What do you want, Mr Mellor?"

"I want to know the truth, not the nonsense you fed me in the Institute, the real truth."

"I don't know."

"Don't, just don't. You wouldn't be the first person I have killed this week, you wouldn't even be the third. No lies, I know the truth around the coding on the letters. I know I am an M&P and my sister is C&L. I know everything."

Dr Smith sat back in his chair. He wasn't going to be able to get out of this one with the normal lines that he fed people.

"What I want to know now is why?"

"Can I say, in the interest of science? Is that an acceptable answer?"

"What, in the interest of science you have made me into a murderer?"

"It is not that simple, the work we are doing could change the whole world. Michael, I don't think you understand. If we are able to recreate the genes that turn people into murderers then maybe we would be able to extract the same gene. What if nobody born ever had the desire to kill a human being? What if we could make a world that removed all negativity and created a positive world?"

"So to be able to do this you messed with hundreds and thousands of us?"

"Some of you already had those genes, Michael, and some we needed to give a little help."

"How? How did you help? What did you do?"

"The long story or the short one?" Michael wasn't up for games.

"In simple terms we accidently discovered something in the lab. We discovered that if we placed a pen in the sperm in the lab and made a clockwise motion, over time the sperm followed the pen, all together at the same speed. If you know how it works between a man and a woman, now that is totally different. When a man ejaculates into a woman it is almost a free for all, all the sperms heading nearly in the same direction but trying to beat each other. We brought uniformity to what was chaos. The result was a young man called Ian Fogerty, a more complying, obliging, polite man you will never meet. We wondered if we had done that."

"And had you?"

"Yes we had. We then started to see what else we could do. We extract the eggs out of a woman and chopped them as small as possible. You couldn't see with the naked eye, but because the sperm couldn't nestle in it any more, it drove it mad, it started to turn on the other sperms and they would take bites out of each other. This was where you came from. We have been experimenting now over forty years and we can manipulate almost any sense or trait."

"You almost look proud of yourself, doctor. It is like you don't care what you have done."

Dr Smith didn't answer. He was proud of his work. This had been his life's work and he even had a patient upstairs. He had made the perfect daughter.

"Fuck me, you are proud of this, you are proud of what you have done to me, what you have done to all of us." Michael's voice was loud now, so loud it had woken Alana and she was coming down the stairs. Alex managed to duck into the kitchen as she passed the hallway and opened the study door.

"And you gave this hard drive to Alex?"

"Yes."

Chris knew now what she was doing, she had obviously figured out two plus two equals Michael. If Michael was on a list she would be hunting him down. She wouldn't allow him to roam free if she knew he was potentially going to kill.

"I am telling the truth, Detective."

"I didn't say you weren't, Dee."

"There is a doubt in both your faces. I can see it."

"It is not doubt, it's disbelief that this is happening, this is the first we knew of any of this."

"As I said, Detective, it is the truth and I can prove it."

"Michael, what are you doing?"

"I am sorry, Alana, I truly am, but this is between your father and me."

"Daddy, what is going on?"

"Come over here with me, it is going to be okay. We are just working through a few things."

"No, you sit over there in that chair, Alana."

Alana didn't know which way to turn but Michael had the gun. He had planned to torture Dr Smith to get the information out of him but he was willingly telling him everything that had happened. Alana sat in the chair.

"So what now, Michael, I have told you how and why we are doing what we are doing, what now?"

"You haven't told me why, you have said in the name of science, how is what you have done to me in the name of science?"

"Dad, what is he talking about? What have you done to him?"

Michael looked directly at Alana. She doesn't know, she doesn't know what her dad has done.

"Your dad has been making experiments in his lab and one of them is me?"

"Dad, is this true?"

"It is not as simple as that, Alana."

"But, Dad, I was born in the lab."

"Yes, you were, you were a perfect healthy baby."

"I bet she was, what did you give her? Some compassion, loyalty, love. Little girls are really made out of sugar and spice, aren't they? And tell her what you gave me. Psychopathic tendencies and murderous ones."

Alana was just staring directly at her father now. "What is he saying, Dad, did you do something to me also?"

Alana started to think that he had, he had done something to her that enabled her to attract lunatics for one. Dr Smith sat silent, he didn't want to say any more.

"You didn't know that Daddy had made you, did you? And not made you in the way you thought. He experimented on you and made you into a perfect little princess. It was just me, me whose life he ruined. But you, no, you his daughter, his perfect little daughter, he couldn't bring to do anything nasty to you." Michael was unravelling again, Alex could hear him through the door; he was projecting his guilt and blame onto someone else.

"No, no harm would ever come to his perfect little daughter."

Alex knew that was the time to get in there but it was too late. By the time she had come through the door three shots had hit Alana square in the chest. Michael hadn't expected her or seen her coming. Before he knew it the gun was out of his hand and he was on his back, on the floor. Alex was above him, gun in hand.

"What do you mean you can prove it?"

"I know I shouldn't have but I copied the hard drive."

Chris and James were both now on their feet. "Where is the copy, Dee?"

"It is on my PC. I wasn't really interested in what was on it at first, but then I got to thinking, what if I met another one, another person that had been born in the Institute, would I want to know first? And every time I thought about it I convinced myself I would. You understand I am not over Jack, but should I want to move on one day, I want to be sure."

"Can we see it?"

"Yes, of course."

Dee got up and went over to the computer, she switched it on and they waited for it to boot up.

"I do have another confession to make. I used it this week."

"To check on a potential date? Or someone you know?"

"No, I will show you."

Dee logged in and opened the file. There were indeed rows of names and addresses just as she had explained. "I was watching the news about those murders upstate, and that a policewoman had been involved. I don't know why but I got the sense it was Alex. That being the case, when they released the names…" Dee typed in Deacon James into the computer. "See, he was in there, he was one of the children from the Brown Institute."

Chris and James were watching in disbelief. "Dee, can you type in the name Oliver Gordon?"

"Yes, sure."

Dee typed in the name and up it came as if it was a phone directory.

"That is it, that's exactly how she knew he was the murderer. Alex is out there with a list of murderers."

"That's not just it, Alex is out there alone with a list of murderers whom she is hell bent on catching."

Dr Smith was holding his daughter as she was bleeding to death. Her wounds weren't going to heal, she had a matter of minutes before the end and blood had started to spurt from her mouth.

"Alex?"

"Yes, Michael. Alex."

"But how?"

"But how did I get here? I followed you, I knew you would go to the Institute, I stayed in the same hotel as you and then I followed you on your little date."

"More criminal than police now then."

Alex knew she was, she wasn't a policewoman any more. She was on the side of right, just not on the side of the law. Michael jumped towards her; she took him down with a single shot to the head. She had fulfilled her contract with Christopher. Michael was dead. More importantly to her she had avenged the murders of Paul's family, his parents and his brother and if anyone asked she had already projected Sophie's murder onto him.

"Thank you. I was convinced he was going to kill me too."

Alex had almost forgot about Dr Smith and the fact he had just seen that.

"Don't thank me, Doctor; it was you that created him. I was just helping to clean up your mess."

"She is gone. He has killed my little girl."

"I am sorry for your loss, but can I ask you a question? Was she one of them? Was she one of the children of the Brown Institute?"

The doctor didn't really want to respond to Alex, but she had just killed a man in front of him.

"Yes."

"Why would you do that to your own daughter? What did she have?"

"Nothing bad, nothing. Compassion, loyalty."

Dr Smith had started to cry. He had lost his little girl to this, his little princess.

"Why, doctor? Why have you done what you have done?"

Dr Smith didn't answer. There were a multitude of reasons why, none of which were going to bring his daughter back and none of which he was allowed to discuss.

As Alex sat there looking at him on the floor she could feel herself getting angrier and angrier at him. All in all Michael hadn't been wrong to come here. Michael hadn't been wrong to want answers from this man. He was a monster. He and his lab had created so many more monsters in the name of science. That couldn't be right. He couldn't get away with this.

"How many?"

The doctor looked up at Alex.

"How many?"

"How many what?"

"How many monsters have you created in the name of science?"

Dr Smith didn't answer.

Alex pulled her gun back out of the holster and pointed directly at him. "How many?"

"I don't know."

"How many, Dr Smith?"

"A hundred thousand maybe, maybe a little more."

A single shot ended Dr Smith's career in the baby and monster making business. Alex couldn't let him live any more. Something had to stop the machine and this is where it started. Alex stood staring at three bodies on the floor. She had seen eleven dead bodies within a week. It was now becoming a daily event. But not one she could deal with easily. She walked over and sat in the doctor's chair as her knees began to buckle underneath her. As she did, on the desk was a case, the same case that Christopher Mellor had brought in when they were in the apartment in Rome.

She opened the case and it was the same device, the tracking device that he had used to find Michael. That was too much of a coincidence; Christopher and the doctor having the same device. As it opened, a box appeared on the front of the screen. Alex remembered it needed a thumb print to be able to open. She stood up and walked over to the doctor. Taking Alana off his lap she pulled him over to the desk and placed his thumb on the screen. It unlocked. She dropped the body where it was and stood looking at the screen. There was a box that said simply 'criteria'.

Alex thought about it, she wondered what the criteria was. Then she remembered the files; the most common, M&P, she typed it in. When she did she remained looking at the screen.

She took the phone Christopher had given her out of her pocket and rang the number. One of his men answered. "Hello?"

"Get him."

"Mr Mellor is in bed."

"Get him now!"

The phone went silent. Alex was fixed to the screen in front of her. After a few minutes a voice came back on the line. "Mr Mellor is here."

"Put him on."

"I am sure you understand."

"I said put him on, he doesn't need to talk he just needs to listen."

Christopher put the phone to his ear.

"I know, I know it all. The job is done but we are not. Get to Germany tomorrow."

Alex hung up the phone.

She sat back in the doctor's chair and looked at the screen. Hundreds of thousands of little dots flickered on a map of the world. Christopher hadn't been monitoring Michael and Maria, the Institute had. He just had access. They were all monitored.

Alex needed a plan.